THE FLEA MARKET TRIBE

THE FLEA MARKET TRIBE
LAURA EVANESKI

ITI Music Corporation

ITI Music Corporation Publishing
16057 Tampa Palms Bl West
Tampa, FL 33543

ISBN: 978-0-9995684-6-0
Printed and bound in the United States
Cover Graphics: RoxC LLC
www.roxc.graphics/Roxanne Clapp
Cover Photos: Canva
Author Drawing: Leslie Simpson

To my Husband, Michael for being so much more than my partner for 25 years. Creating with you has been extremely cool. Thank you for being Editor, Publisher, and listening to my endless stories.

To my Daughter, her husband, and my "grands," you keep me moving forward. Love you all

To my Sisters, Brother by choice and Nephew...new phone..who dis?

To My Mom, thank you for encouraging me to write.

The Flea Market Tribe

"Introduction"

The rest of us in Row G were pretty awestruck. The goal of any professional garage sale or flea market dweller is gold.

Finding a piece of shiny metal laying amongst department store castoff's or aunt Sarah's feather earrings from the late 1970s is the treasure you want.

That bracelet or ring that you instantly know is worth $200 found in some old dress pocket. You know that there are no other items that have that type of a profit margin.

So when Karen in Row F was selling off $1000 to $6000 a week in gold, we possibly could be doing something wrong or were we?

It has happened a few times for me that I found a piece I was able to buy for $20 and flip for $200, but none of us had Karen's kind of luck.

The Flea Market Tribe
Chapter One

"Maine"

The weather in Maine was warming up quickly for April,
not something we were used to.

Heading up to my camp, a one bedroom cabin with an
empty loft with a mesmerizing view of the lake, I thought
about the things I wanted to do there.

I want to garden and have a self-sufficient lifestyle.

These are the dreams I have carried with me my whole life.

This year I was going to attempt to become a year-round
resident.

I am working on my cabin myself and learning to repair
and upgrade the necessary things that go wrong in a 100-
year-old camp. It is not an easy job.

My pellet stove is my pride and joy. I saved for it and
researched it endlessly.

One of the things that drew me to this camp was the almost
circular living room. There are nights in front of the TV
with the stove blazing that I choose to rest my weary bones,
exactly where they are planted.

I don't have a lot of material things which is odd for a
picker, and a seller of wares.

I may keep a find for a short while if it really calls to me and then one day I'll pluck it from the room, and it's off to market.

I guess I never really fall in love with treasures. The only things I choose to collect, alongside my flea market tribe are the stories and experiences from the road.

I woke early to the smell of spring through my window left slightly ajar.

Though my home is on two floors, the loft is for the young, in my opinion. When I'm gone, my son and his family can change it or sell it.

I recently had spoken with Peyton or I should I say he had the talk with me, the last time he came to visit.

"Mom, what do you want?"

I smiled and asked, "Like now?"

Peyton looked at me and said, "No, when you are gone? Do you want to be buried or cremated?"

"Cremated," I stated, "But no urn. I don't want you to carry me around. Put me in a biodegradable box and throw me overboard."

Peyton wasn't amused and said, "But I will not have anyplace to go and visit you."

I said, "Son, you'll carry me in your heart, and every time you see a body of water, you'll say...yo Mom, wassup?"

Peyton just shook his head, but it was settled for now.

The Flea Market Tribe
Chapter Two

"Living in Two Places"

I returned earlier than normal from my Snowbird retreat in Sarasota, Florida, this time. Every year I find another motorhome to rent for the winter.

When you're staying in the RV park of retired folks, it seems that there is always someone who is not well enough to make it down for the winter. Rather than it sits empty, I'm able to help a friend out as much as they are helping me out and at a reduced rate.

I've gained a good reputation amongst this group of friends in Florida, that I have never been RV-less in the last 20 years.

"The frugality girls?" Yes, I need to start a club, thinking to myself.

According to all accounts, the markets this year were a lot slower than in the past. The youngsters, "the millennials," want nothing that their parents before them collected. No glassware for sure!

I'm in sync with them as I have said before, my personal style is minimalist.

If you got a favorite sweatshirt, you don't need five that are similar. Things are always replaceable, most of what we have in life are just things!

I do enjoy the garage sales in Sarasota as I seem to find unique trinkets and other items that will sell at the local markets. If it doesn't, it comes home with me to Maine.

Home... Maine is home. My humble place amongst the trees. My kitchen is a patchwork of utensils and dinnerware that fit like a well-worn puzzle.

In a corner sits my apartment size black and white Wedgewood stove, naturally distressed vintage side boy that has become the replacement for shelving and cabinets.

I had to pull the existing ones off the walls as they were falling apart, (enter arthritis), as it seems this was exactly the arrival of my pain issues.

The vintage four seat dining table is quite worn with white, black, and silver accents. If I remember correctly, this came from the diner in the middle of town.

A few red vintage Fiestaware pieces brighten up the kitchen, which is simple but lovely.

My dishes and cookbooks are carefully displayed on the buffet cabinets. The knobs are a collection I had saved for years after buying them from a variety of estate and garage sales.

They are all different and mostly have to do with Maps. Though I don't know how to read a map, I've always collected things that show them. In fact, my prize possession is a map of the Hawaiian Islands. This now collectible piece is worth several hundred dollars, so my husband had it placed in an expensive frame for one of my birthdays.

The back room has a stackable washer dryer I purchased off craigslist, with shelves that I use as a pantry.

The invisible type barn door that a friend found on the side of the road installed it that brings light into the small kitchen when opened.

Another prize possession that I found one day sifting through a barn was a double-sided farmhouse sink that has seen several generations along with the spoons, forks, and knives that were used to feed these people.

The small bedroom has a desk and a laptop for Internet sales and a bed.

My walls are covered sparingly with framed prints from Bristol Rhythm and Roots. These were gifted to me by the Birthplace of Country Music and always have been part of my special treasures.

The truth be told I rarely use the bed in this room and save it for company, as I prefer my cozy living room couch in front of my pellet stove.

This week is the start of a few estates and indoor tag sales, as it is still a little too early for the flea markets to open.

I am preparing and tagging items, as well as doing research on my offerings. My handmade tags show the history of the item and where it was found if at all possible.

I am meeting up later with my friends Lee and Gayle to discuss our winters, and of course our finds, and any local news.

I chose these two as friends because they are no bullshit gals, much like myself. I have chosen poorly in the past as far as friends go, so I am very cautious now at my age.

I have never found gossip an enduring quality and try to surround myself with like minds.

Later in the day, I met up with the ladies. They told me that Lee's son who is a police officer in our town had been dealing with the drug epidemic that normally doesn't cross borders into this small hamlet where families have owned their land for hundreds of years.

Unfortunately, it has brought along other crimes such as burglaries and automobile break-ins.

Her son Bobby told her to be extra vigilant, using that old motto – "see something say something."

Bobby also trained us over the years to use handguns and made sure that we received our concealed carry permits just to make sure we were safe. Needless to say, we're all damn good shots.

We met in town at a restaurant that caters to all, including a great vegan option that I enjoy.

On our table, we spread out the local newspaper called "Zine" and started to plot out our days for any sales to attend during the week.

I enjoy estate sales but only ones run by a family or trustee. Professional estate sale companies tend to overcharge since their split is 60/40 or 50/50. Not exactly profitable for a reseller.

After our lunch and hilarious chat about the locals, I went home and spent the next two weeks preparing my stock for the market's opening.

Then I drove over to my spot to make sure 2G was tidy and swept and ready for selling my finds.

The undercover spot with the horseshoe nailed above it had long ago rusted over and had been there as long as I could remember, but the spot was as ready as it could be.

I was beginning to get excited again, like a child on her first day at school.

The Flea Market Tribe
Chapter Three

"The Market Opens"

Opening day at the market and my truck has been packed
for two days. 3 AM came early, but the excitement was
overwhelming to get back out and do what I love best.

Flea-marketing is a mix of friends and characters. Some, I
keep in touch with via Facebook all winter long.

This year seemed to start a bit slower than usual, as had
been predicted in the local news.

The early morning was full of other vendors looking to
poach something that you didn't know the value of.

Of course, other vendors were snooping around that resell
at the upcoming extravaganza. This event is next month in
another town. It is an all vintage and collectible market,
and these vendors look to source from the flea market.

Then finally, the shoppers arrived, looking for jewelry,
specifically gold.

I was happy to have Gayle and Lee in the same row. We
are like the sisterhood of traveling junk.

My friend Gayle is a well-dressed woman in her late
sixties. She is simple elegance. Never overdone. She has
a sense of humor that tickles me silly. And there is hearty
laughter whenever we are together.

Gayle is British with an accent that I am constantly telling
her that she needs to take her comedy show on the road.

She is my friend, and I am very blessed. She specializes in European vintage and antiquities and is constantly learning and researching, which I admire that about her.

There are a number of people that buy & sell gold. Years ago, when I first started, I would sell all of my gold to Thomas, but once I caught on that Thomas sold his gold to Blaine, I went directly to Blaine. He buys all of the gold from the other gold sellers, so I go to him, to cut out the middleman.

It's day one, and the drama has started already. Karen is already doing her shtick. I'm a jeweler; I will pay the most for your gold, she says with a cigarette hanging off her lip and her ashes falling on some other vendor's table, and merchandise.

When she runs into the few people that actually like her, she insists on kissing them squarely on the mouth. You can see the fear in the person's face as she goes in for that kiss. Personally, I'm throwing up a little bit in my mouth just thinking about it.

Regrettably, my row has some new vendors which happen to be gun dealers. This makes me incredibly uncomfortable.

Mike is set up right next to me. He is of some foreign descent, and I am unsure from where.

Frustrated in setting up his space, he begins telling me my tables are over the line.

After I schooled him on the rules, he is pretty enraged.

"Nice start to the day bozo," I say to myself.

I'm well known for turning my stock quickly. I often tell customers this is not a traveling museum; everything is for sale, including my displays. I can always replenish and I rarely refuse a decent offer.

I tend to cross-list items online that includes eBay, Etsy, Mecari, and Poshmark. If something sells at the flea market or on any of these sites, I quickly remove it from the other sites.

It really is a win-win, since it means I have so many more eyes on the item. I, therefore, give my online sites to my prospective customers at the flea market. This is called cross-marketing.

I would consider today a soft opening as there was a smaller crowd than normal.

The day brought some good sales and a few new finds, though I had to deal with my new neighbor, "the gunrunner."

Yes, I was bothered by him, but I also ended up giving him a few suggestions, after watching him sell guns all day without checking identification.

I told him that he might want to move his spot as there was a pretty good connection to a few ATF officers by some of the old time vendors.

Not to be put off by him, at any rate, it was good to be back at my happy place.

As I packed up my truck, my mind wandered to the past when and where I worked a somewhat traditional life. All be it, one of a music executive.

I did enjoy my career, but I never set out to work in that field, I just kind of fell into it.

Like my favorite singer songwriter's lyric "distracted" by Ani DiFranco, I spent a great many years, working freelance before taking a more corporate position. I would say the only thing that I missed about it was the steady paycheck. Knowing that every two weeks "x amount" of money would be deposited was always reassuring.

Between this and the fact that my husband was retired, I was smart enough and able to put it all away and lived off my extracurricular activity money, "side hustle."

I learned more than I could imagine, but I also learned what and who I wanted to be and who I most definitely did not want to be.

I think that is what led me to this life in Maine, having spent my whole life being who other people wanted me to be.

While I lived my life for my husband and son, which was probably noble, it left little time actually to define who Jillian was.

With our son grown and my husband Nickolas deciding that he wanted to spend much of his days traveling from one country to another, to follow his own bliss, it was time for me.

Much older than me, he writes books and creates music. Before that he spent his life as a military officer, a "Mustang" in fact.

During those years, he worked hard to take care of our family as much as I did. But this was his life, where his military career kept us apart, a great deal of time, living in other countries, including Spain & Italy which are two that come to mind.

That was in a way our business. But now it's personal for me. A huge history buff, Nick is driven to not only see people and places but to investigate every aspect of them.

I, on the other hand, have no interest. Though we clearly love each other and consider ourselves happily married.

Quite spoiled as he entered his seventies, trim, tan and handsome, Nick likes nice hotels, festive meals and enjoys good wine. Where I had unfortunately been dealing with the midlife spread, some medical issues, was celebrating over 11 years of sobriety, thank you, God!

A gypsy at heart. Very frugal. I love to dig through other people's junk and am willing to stop at the side of the road for a castoff.

Proud to have done this, I have dug through a few too many dumpsters in my day, in spite of suffering from anxiety which I try not to let hinder me too much.

As a couple, we are affording each other the simple pleasure of being our own authentic selves, and it has worked out fine.

The Flea Market Tribe
Chapter Four

"Sister Trips"

That evening I made a meal of salad and cold beets, which is my favorite along with my go-to beverage of lemon Lacroix over chipped ice, and fresh lemon and lime wedges.

Then I sat on my spot in front of my warm pellet stove, organizing my colorful vintage bead collection and making bracelets.

Mostly from traveling alone, I started this fun game years ago while working in the business world. If I am wearing a piece of jewelry that I had made, and complemented by an associate or friend, I would take it off and gift it to them.

Imagine my surprise when I found out that after being complimented by another friend, they would, in turn, continue my tradition of gifting the bracelet.

So being a loving gesture, not only do I stock a selection in my booth but keep some on hand for gifting. Plus when I find less than desirable vintage jewelry that still has special beads intact, I add them to my collection.

I like to be a generous woman. I grew up with very selfish parents, and I sought out to be as different from them as possible. My Father was selfish with his time, and my Mother was just busy.

Fortunately, the only thing really good that came out of my childhood were my sisters.

It has taken us over half our lives to come together, to trust one another after being gaslighted for most of our upbringing and adulthood.

So finally, after all these years, we started the sister trips.

We would meet up somewhere for a few days to "be still" and safe within our sweet sister cocoon.

Our youngest sister's husband sometimes comes as well since we adore him and consider him kind of a sister. He has the biggest and most generous heart of anyone I know and is pretty shy about taking praise.

The sister trips soothe my soul. They all like to kid me about my frugal nature, telling me that I should write a book about the ways to live, and by being a good steward of God's blessings.

On my last flight, I started packing only a carry-on and hand washing a couple of pairs of pants I brought. At the gate, they offered to check my luggage through to my final destination at no charge. Whoop-de-do! I love that. Thirty dollars saved!

Now, these days many airports have water filling stations for your reusable bottles (rather than buying the $5.00 Dasani water) they sell in the airport store. Nothing chaps my hide more than paying for a water brand I dislike, and it's only filtered tap water.

Here's a trick for all you travelers. Bring a Tervis coffee cup with lid. Ask any restaurant in the airport for a cup of ice. They won't mind giving it to you if you're not asking for a cup. You can add the ice to your water or vice-versa as it always tastes better when it's cold.

I also need the coffee cup to use in the hotel for that 2nd cup to take on the road.

I learned that trick after years of convention life. I've also been known to carry a Ziploc bag to bring back dinner to my room. I think we all get a little weird or smarter in our old age.

But I'm getting ahead of myself, and it's not sister trip time just yet.

When I awoke, I needed a strong cup of coffee and prepped up my French press. When my husband is home, he's in charge of blending our coffee, but when he's not here, I do it my way.

The mornings are still cold, and my fire keeps everything toasty.

The flea market opens at 7 am on Sunday, so I am soon on my way for day number two of my weekly journey.

By the time I get set up at my booth, the market is abuzz with news about the local break-ins.

It seems a family up on Pine Ridge almost walked smack dab into a burglar last night while returning from a family wedding.

Sharon Mossbank, the wife, lost all of her gold jewelry as she had chosen to wear a costume matching pearl set, she had bought from the shopping channel.

Lee came by and said her son Bobby told her, though they caught the punks, there was another break in later in the night, so they were certain they were dealing with more than one group. The robbery at the camp took the families silver service that had been passed down through the generations.

Obviously, it had to be drug-related as both of these things hit our town simultaneously.

Lee and I assured Bobby we would be vigilant. He warned us not to flash any high-end jewelry or cash as you never knew who had their eye on you.

I asked Bobby, "If there was anything, he could do about Mike, the gun dealer?"

I went on to say, "I was watching him sell 30 plus guns a day, without cases that he wrapped in a plastic grocery bag like some cartel passing off the goods."

Bobby flat out told me, "Mind your own business, please, and I will look into it."

Never been a fan of someone telling me to mind my own business, I thought to myself laughing out loud, then said, "Yes Sir!"

The Flea Market Tribe
Chapter Five

"The Auctions"

Another way of scouting for merchandise are at good old fashion auctions.

Things to expect:
*You are going to pay an auction fee on top of your winning bid.
*You are going to pay tax unless you have a resale tax document.
*Unless you have a relationship with the auctioneer, you're not going to win. He or she has their favorites and are simply going to say they didn't see you. Unless of course, no one else wants the lot, (then you win).

Table-lots:
If you see three things, you can flip on a table lot; the rest is gravy. If you are selling on multiple online sites, you can maximize your sell-through.

#1- Some auctioned items are procured by the auction house themselves.
#2- Pickers bring in lots for the auction. You're not likely to get many surprises in these. These folks know what they are doing.
#3- Estates. These can be fun, and some treasures can be found. However, normally the items are spread out on large tables, with junk that you will want to dispose of.

Today was successful for me as I found a large lot of costume jewelry, including pins and many of the pieces were signed Juliana. I was certain I could turn these items.

I also picked a lot no one was interested in, patches. Some old "new stock" (vintage items that are new but have never been in circulation), as well as some vintage work patches and name tags. These were at the bottom of the box, and no one noticed them. They can be quite lucrative.

The winning bid on this lot was five dollars, but I projected the outcome of the sale to be closer to $500.

Tuesday, I spent working in my greenhouse garden and listing my auction purchases.

I made fresh marinara from the garden, and after it simmered all day, I canned the rest the next morning.

Later, Lee, Gayle, and I went to a free movie in town. We are all such suckers for a love story, as we watched "The Notebook" for likely the 25th time. There we sat, three older ladies with three large handbags full of munchies.

As we drove Gayle home and up her driveway, we noticed a light flicker on her sunporch. Something felt out of place.

Lee immediately called her son Bobby and asked to have someone come by before we went inside the house.

Within three minutes flat Bobby was there in an unmarked car along with another police vehicle. While the police went in to check out the house with Gayle's key, we waited outside.

After Bobby came back outside, he told us that someone had definitely broken in but hadn't gotten very far as we must've come home just in time.

We were all shocked but went into the house with Gayle to see if anything was missing after the officers determined the house as safe.

Gayle said she didn't notice if anything was missing, after looking throughout the house and checking her valuables.

Afterward, Bobby said, "Stay safe and sharp ladies and drove off."

When Gayle was done, we went outside and sat on the front porch to make sure that Gayle felt at ease.

Gayle and Lee both had a small glass of bourbon, and I drank my club soda. Meanwhile, an officer was parked in the front yard making sure all was well. That's certainly the difference in a small town, I guess. People actually care about your well-being.

The Flea Market Tribe
Chapter Six

"The Drama Begins"

Saturday morning came quickly, after such a chaotic week, with the break-in.

Friday turned into a pretty good day since there were a few estate sales and tag sales.

Gayle recovered too, since nothing had been taken in the robbery attempt, so she was very excited to have found a beautiful 18 karat gold pin.

She decided to sell it to Thomas, as it would help pay for the new security system that she was having installed, not that Smith and Wesson wasn't good enough.

Then Gayle came over to my booth and asked me, "Can you come with me for a moment?"

I told her, "Sure" and followed her over to the gold buyer as he was busy waiting on another customer.

Gayle whispered to me, "Isn't that the ring you bought me for my birthday sitting in that pile next to his scale?"

She told me that it was sitting in a small dish on her kitchen counter and she did not realize it was missing. But I knew that there could not be two rings like that and just said, "Yep!"

I then told her not to say anything as we needed to find out what was going on. And how in the hell did a missing ring

21

from her house, after a break-in, show up at the flea market?

When the day was done, after the market, Lee took Gayle to the police station to see Bobby.

The ring at Thomas's booth did not make sense. So the women wanted to report it as soon as possible.

Meanwhile, in the less desirable part of town, deceptively the drug cartel was checking into the only two hotels in town. These hotels were similar and owned by two sisters.

The hotels were quaint and these two guys stuck out like sore thumbs.

For the record, it is a well-known fact that when drugs play a part, crime goes hand-in-hand.

In the interim, both Lee and I helped Gayle out with the extra money that she needed for the security system. We were worried about our friend, as the robbery could have happened to any of us.

The days that followed seemed to calm down a little bit. We were vigilant, but we went back to doing what we do.

I would say that our little group was even a bit tighter knit than usual, with safety in numbers.

Nonetheless, knowing that Peyton, his wife, and my two grandsons, we're coming into town the following Tuesday, I was beside myself with excitement.

My son and his wife were taking the spare bedroom, while my four-year-old grandsons would cuddle with Grammy on the couch.

Peyton is very much a family man, and I was extremely proud of who he had become. His younger days saw a lot of partying while in college, and I sometimes wondered if he was going to make the cut and graduate.

When he broke up with his college sweetheart, everything seemed to change. He later told me that the relationship ended because she felt he was not marriage material.

Though I adored the young woman he dated for so many years, I knew in my heart that Julia was meant to come into his life, after he became a responsible mature and ready man.

I still had the weekend and Monday to get through, as I returned my attention to the current events.

The market was bustling with people getting back in town.

Folks were bringing their wares from wherever they had spent their winter. There were a lot of newbies, with people selling their garage sale items to boot.

The folks that had just returned were astounded about the recent crime wave.

Not many people knew that there were drug issues in town. However, us three women who were in the know because of Bobby were kept apprised of the situation.

We were still pretty baffled, trying to figure out how Gayle's ring ended up in a pile of gold on the table of

Thomas, since he sells gold and other metals directly to the refinery guy, Blaine.

So with Blaine now in possession of Gayle's ring, the question was, "How do we get it back?"

Something very strange was going on in this tiny town with a population of less than a thousand, I thought.

"Why here. What makes this town a place to rob people?"

The following morning, I spent working in my garden, where I grow my hydroponic Romaine and small English cucumbers along with tomatoes that screamed, "Salad! Salad!" It was one of the goals that I had since moving here and calling this my home and be my own woman and fend for myself.

Another day rolled by and a weekday estate sale brought a vintage accordion style wooden sewing box from Romania, that I paid five dollars for and will sell it between 50 and 60 dollars. Far below retail, but ready to turn it fast.

There is nothing more exciting than buying merchandise for the market or from online, though selling online, I would prefer to ship only small items.

Today the estate sale was close to home. I didn't find much but a tall clear container, filled with silver chains, caught my eye.

However, as I looked through the container, the bony shape of a woman appeared, and the booming voice of Karen and her cigarette drawl bellowed loud and clear, "I'm getting those silver chains," she yelled at me.

Though the chains are currently in my hands, I am surprised when Karen steps in front of me and yanks the plexiglass container away from me.

But I am not amazed as nothing ever is with her. So after she walks out the door, I chuckle and say to the estate sale leader, "I still have this heavy nice herringbone chain in my hand" (which was the best piece of the lot).

Smiling back at me, the estate sales company owner says, "Looks like she just bought you a pretty necklace!"

"I will enjoy selling this piece," I replied with a silly grin that showed my amusement.

The next two days were fast and furious with my children and grandchildren in tow. We spent a great deal of time outside, hanging in the hammock, barbecuing, and enjoying each other's company. When they left on that second day at exactly 4 PM, I missed them already as they pulled out of the driveway.

However, I rewarded myself during that still cool night, in front of my pellet stove, feeling hopeful for the antique and vintage show the next day.

Heading out in the morning, I opted to visit another location purely for research to see if this was the show, I might look into exhibiting my wares?

As I left at the crack of dawn, I came across two separate herds of deer.

As Blake Shelton's "God's Country" softly played from the radio, I couldn't help but feel like I was experiencing something magical.

Sometimes there are those moments in your life like driving through the Blue Ridge Mountains where you actually feel you've experienced something bigger than yourself. This was kind of like that moment.

Once while on my way for business to Bristol TN/VA, my plane had to make an emergency landing in Spartanburg SC. After checking the flight schedules, I decided to drive the rest of the way through the incredible rolling hills, mountains, and greenery that was everywhere, rather than wait for a flight the next day that took you into the small twin cities airport outside of town.

I spent the entire drive crying. It was so breathtaking.

Since then, I have taken many trips to Bristol, and it will always be a special place for me. Down the main street, there is a double yellow line. One side is Tennessee and the other side in Virginia.

I once asked a policeman on Main street if there was an accident who would be responsible Police Officer in either Tennessee or Virginia?

His reply with a smile on his face was, "Whatever side the car ends up on!"

Truly wonderful memories.

The town alive with the festival every year called Bristol Rhythm and Roots Reunion. There are three days and more than forty bands or artists that appear.

The merchandise area is in an old hundred-year-old furniture store with incredible staircases and metal tile ceilings.

I think I was immediately in love with that store with its
large display windows. Very spectacular & enchanting.

You could see an artist one year just as they were on the
verge of stardom, but they would be back again bigger than
life, the following year, as this festival was true hometown
and fans and artists alike made the most of the annual party.

At home, I sat at my desk drinking hot tea and looking
through a small tin of gemstones and possible diamonds.

When I had walked by the gold booth at the market the
other day, as usual, the ground was sparkling.

The refineries care nothing about the stones, so the gold
buyers pop all of them out of the jewelry before making a
sale to the big refinery guy. Some of these gemstones can
be quite large in size and ultimately worth a good nickel or
two.

I definitely needed to get my new "finds" checked out since
I knew that I could resell them.

Interesting enough while I was digging around on the
ground, a young man walked over to me and asked me
what I was doing?

I told him that I was finding treasure on the ground. He
asked me if he could join in. Not only did I say yes, but I
gifted him one of the little tins I was using.

He thought it was such a blast and when his friend came
looking for him, he was like "dude I got diamonds!"

It is the simplicity of life. Isn't it?

I think that's one of the reasons I love what I do. Trust me; I am not getting rich. And there have been days I question my sanity and my business plan, but at the end of the day, it really does bring me joy. The conversations that I have with people almost seem unbelievable.

I was gifted a really cool print this past week from the record guy and his wife, Hope. It's called the "Flea Market Blues, and it's a drawing of an old blues singer and his flea market booth jamming. The print had fallen, and the glass was broken.

When he gave it to me, he said, "Here, you can have this. I know you like weird things. I was going to give it to my friend Johnny, but I think you'd enjoy it more."

Back home, checking my Mercari store for any leads, my phone rang, and it was Gayle letting me know that Lee's house had been robbed. The police, including Bobby, were all there, and Gayle was going to swing by my camp to pick me up.

How screwed up is this? Whoever is doing this is likely not from this area because everyone knows that Lee is Bobby's mother and no local would have anything to do with pissing off Bobby Burgess.

When Gayle arrived at my house, you could tell she was likely ready for bed when she got the call. Freshly scrubbed face and a housecoat and hot tea and her Tervis cup.

Once we rounded the corner, we were met with the barrage of police lights. They extended the length of the street.

It seems that two houses were hit, Lee and her neighbor Bob Tarbert, who lived a few houses down the road.

Well, I expected Lee to be upset; however, what I found was her pissed off beyond measure. She was outraged, and I could understand. Some of the jewelry that was taken included the substantial gold coin jewelry that she had been collecting for many years.

Lee said to me, "Guess your next! Gayle and I have already been hit."

Lee also thought it was less about connection and simply out of coincidence, but my mind kept going to Gayle's ring that ended up on Thomas's table.

Gayle drove me home, and we were quiet along the way back to my place. I hugged her goodbye and went inside, and after a hot shower, I popped into bed, but my mind was on the flea market tribe.

The Flea Market Tribe
Chapter Seven

"The Tribe"

In anthropology, a tribe is a human social group. The
concept is often contrasted with other social group concepts
such as nations, states, and forms of kinship. Thank you,
Wikipedia!

Lee was busy with the insurance issues, and Gayle and I
went over to help her put her house back together. We
thought it was the best thing that we could do to make her
feel more comfortable in her own home.

As the week flew by, "The Tribe" was back at the flea
market before we knew it.

Standing at my booth, I saw Karen speaking to a police
officer as she claimed someone had stolen six thousand
dollars out of her car. The stories were fast and furious as
someone else said she was walking around earlier through
two rows saying that she lost a bag of gold...

Karen had reported the theft, but I could see her husband
out in a smaller field with his picking partner. As for his
picking partner, he looked more like a thug, but I have yet
to figure that out.

One of the sellers told me that he seems to be under the
influence of drugs. I'm normally skeptical of what other
sellers tell me unless it's my own group as people have
issues and will constantly tell tales if you listen.

I went by Thomas, the gold buyer's booth, and he seemed a
bit on edge and told me, "if you have any gold to sell he

was buying, as it had been slow for him and he wanted and needed to make some money.

The hair on the back of my neck stood straight up. WTF?

With the amount of gold going through this booth, this made zero sense.

"Pace yourself," I thought, things are about to get real.

Meanwhile, I'm trying to concentrate on my own booth and sales to make a living, rather than being a character out of "Colombo" or "Murder She Wrote."

The market this year contains many different types of sellers. After the whole closet "clean out" craze of 2018, people were done with clutter, and the national thrift stores were the recipient for all of this overindulgence.

Well, this seems like a great idea, but there are several problems to this. One of them is that thrift shops don't sell children's toys, which is funny since children's toys come in by the carloads.

These toys then find themselves in the same place that the soccer Mom with three kids and a minivan full of donations feared most. The dumpster.

"Minivan Mom" doesn't realize that this thrift store doesn't sell children items, such as toys and strollers, because they can't keep up with the recalls. I know many folks that have made a living out of this thrift stores dumpster and then reselling it at the Flea Market.

This is the best possible news as it's not ending up in the landfill, and hopefully, some underprivileged family is benefiting off the incredibly low price.

I know another man that has made between 68 to 80 grand a year picking the other national chains dumpster of phones, laptops, other electronics, and many other items. He states this one store in another town, dumps 25-30 percent of all donations.

The situation is even more dire than that. The US government estimates that more than 85% of the textiles that are discarded every year end up in the landfills.

Furthermore, donation boxes have popped up in every parking lot across America, and in many cases, you have no idea who manages it or what interest it serves.

Some of the big box stores actually sell, clothes, and shoes that are in good shape in their stores and online. Much of the rest is packaged into bales, that is sold cheaply by the pound or auctioned off to overseas distributors, intended for destinations in Asia, Africa, and Latin America.

There is a company called Recycle Match that currently offers 42,000 pounds of winter clothes per month for three cents a pound and 20,000 pounds of sneakers and tennis shoes per month for $.19 per pound.

A common misconception is that old clothes donated are often freely distributed to developing countries, in the recycle clothing boxes that you see in parking lots for donations.

Clothes are recycled by being sold overseas, and more than 50% are incinerated or end up in landfills.

Not the idea you have when dropping off that minivan load of blessings, I suppose.

So maybe flea markets and garage sales are a good thing as these items are purchased by someone who needs it or a reseller that is looking to flip it.

Maybe just delaying its detour to the landfill for a short time helps, but one can hope.

Meanwhile, this week, there was a break in the case of Lee's stolen jewelry. Then there was a raid on the two small hotels in town. The ones in which police were concerned that some of this new drug trade had infiltrated.

With search warrants served, they recovered some of Lee's gold coin pieces.

So what was feared had become a reality, this was everything to do with drugs.

Now everyone was chatting it up at our one and only coffee shop in town.

I sat with Lee, Bobby, and Gayle. Our table was the place to stop as everyone wanted to have a conversation with Bobby and find out what was going on in town.

Of course, he tried to put everyone's mind at rest and that this was just something that was going on, and it would be cleared up quickly.

People were positively fearful, and Ron's Gun Shack was doing a brisk business this morning, or so it was rumored.

Many stories were going around, and we were just trying to be tightlipped until we knew what the real story was.

Even the yard sales were buzzing with conversations regarding break-ins and drug issues. And people were certainly acting strange, though not sure if it was out of fear?

Gayle told us that she saw Karen at a yard sale, having a big fight with Joe, who owns the local pawn shop in town.

Joe always told his customers that "This pawnshop is probably more like a thrift or resale store."

I would have to agree with Joe since he is always turning over his inventory.

But the sign still says "pawnshop," which is more manly, when you think about it.

Not sure what they were fighting about but it was serious enough for Gayle to let us know. Everyone knows she's not my favorite person.

Following this, we went our separate ways, and I spent the early part of my week in my garden. One of my places of Solace trying to ensure a good crop to last me through the fall and winter should I decide to stay this year.

I enjoyed my craft project of mosaic pieces from floral plates and broken Fiestaware.

Creating a colorful bench to sit on, I am using an old wooden bench I pulled off the side of the road.

I plan to cover the entire thing as a mosaic except for the seating area top and bottom. The turquoise cushions will add softness to the seating arrangement.

Last year my project was creating the fire pit. As vast and scary looking, a fire can be, it is also very soothing.

I remember when my son was a young toddler, and we would fall asleep on the floor near the fireplace to keep warm on bitterly cold nights.

The Flea Market Tribe
Chapter Eight

"Karen and Thomas"

The market is positively filled with characters such as
Karen. One thing that I noticed this year was the difference
in Karen. Her desperation level was gone.

Karen was not looking at the mess she had made of her life.
She only thought about five minutes ahead if that.

Her husband was always involved in one scam or another.
Most of the time it was bad checks for merchandise that the
two of them bought at garage sales.

Karen knew that this time, she was in a far deeper than
usual. Having people contact your kids through Facebook
trying to get paid on a bad check was one thing. Having
two separate police business cards stuck between the crack
of your front door was an uncomfortable situation.

She knew that she was living a dangerous life these days,
which she didn't mean to get in as deep as she did. She
really didn't see a way out as she put the clear gallon size
Ziploc bags full of gold and jewelry, silverware in a
recyclable shopping bag.

After the police showing up, she knew she had to get the
bag out of the house but to where?

Her husband started out dabbling in and selling
Methamphetamine and heroin and graduated to just about
everything, including Oxycodone, Xanax were just a few
things he offered.

When Karen went to the flea market, she met up with Thomas to properly and quietly move the highly prized metals.

With the influx of the drugs on the outskirts of town, it quickly put her life on blast. A quiet little hustle had turned into something so much bigger and so much scarier.

What Karen knew was twofold, crime spiked when the drug culture took over, and the bad guys were breaking into houses stealing valuables mostly gold trading it for drugs.

Karen knew that she and her husband were supplying some of these drugs and receiving some of this gold. But since the drug cartel had moved in and was running the show, they were ready to remove Karen and her husband from the scenario, which terrified her.

Stealing had never been for Karen, but being a shyster was, and she was very proud of it. However, she never wanted to be known as a drug dealer or even fencing jewelry.

Now the idea was to stay out of the way of the cartel, so they didn't decide to eliminate her and her man. It was a tricky situation, as they were simply and obviously just a small piece of this pie.

Karen met up with Thomas and sold the gold that she had in her possession. Thomas was purely making a taste to move it along up the chain.

She desired to eliminate any evidence that should the police return to Karen's house; there wouldn't be any that they could find, for at least this week.

Even before Thomas saw Karen moving in his direction, he had a sinking feeling in the stomach.

Because he had done some favors in the beginning, he was now being blackmailed and was in too deep himself.

He was taking a huge risk for a very small payout. That is, if you spent $6000 worth of gold at scrap prices, he was lucky to get $500 out of it even though he was only keeping it for a short time, no more than a few hours.

Karen and her husband were stressing him out terribly, and he was popping Tums like they were Lifesavers.

Normal customers for Thomas, other than other flea market sellers, who stopped by to sell and buy their gold, were the only way he was keeping his head above water, financially.

Dealing with Karen and her effervescent smell of nicotine, Thomas often wondered if she showered at all. Overdone in perfume, makeup, jewelry, and flashy clothes, one would think she was channeling ZaZa Gabor!

Thomas truly detested Karen. She's the one who got him involved in this situation in the first place. Meanwhile, he was keeping all of this from his wife, who had bad anxiety issues, and this would be the last thing that he could tell her.

Unbeknownst to anyone else, the thing that drove Karen was the constant fear that her utilities would be shut off or her car payment would bounce.

She was way more social and would spend an hour or so with the gold guy.

And now, with six to eight thousand dollars a week, Thomas had to painstakingly go through each piece of gold that Karen was selling.

Not to be left behind, her husband was well known for being a kleptomaniac seemed to be suddenly, a bon vivant.

Most of us noticed, including the Tribe, that we were seriously not working smart enough if these two bozo's, were being so successful.

Karen's husband walked around with his guy pal, a thug I had mentioned earlier.

As he strolled across the rows of vendors, Freddy carried his "murse," a man's purse, and would tell you what he had inside the bag. It was very revolting to know that this man was born into this life to be such a sleaze!

Karen and I have had so many run-ins that I couldn't even begin to think of her kindly. My upbringing did not prepare me for people like this.

The Flea Market Tribe
Chapter Nine

"Cape Cod"

The New England area of Cape Cod was home to a few
classes of people. One of them was called "The Townies,"
who were the upper class and the other people called
"common trash."

Growing up, I attended Woods Hole High School. Then at
sixteen, I left school at 16 years old to earn a living.
Things were tough.

By the time I was eighteen, I was working in a bar called
"The Captain Kid."

My Father worked for the Oceanographic Center, and my
Mother for an insurance company in town located next
door to a little candy shop.

I still remember that little shop so well because one year
my Mother brought us each a box of Valentine's candy.

The heart-shaped box was filled with white, pink, and red
heart gummies that were sour and soft at the same time.
And I remember it so well because it was so out of
character for my Mom. Generosity was not her strong suit,
and thoughtfulness was not always there.

Likely growing up in Woods Hole, a small fishing town is
why I sought out Maine.

Bartending, particularly as a young woman, was an
education. I learned how to deal with every class of person

and every personality type. I truly believe I would not be the woman I am today, had I not done those things. Street smart, I am business savvy and full of tenacity because, as a young girl, I had fought for my survival.

Over the years those were not things I shared with others. Not because I was embarrassed about not graduating high school. But that I didn't want to glamorize it, since I feel I made it, and not everyone else did.

Though inside somewhere I am sure there is some regret, I relish in the fact that I have no student loans and did a fine job at making a living.

The town of Woods Hole is still quaint to this day. The nearby village of Falmouth, however, had a serious heroin problem, which to me was quite shocking, since I also spent a great deal of time in that town.

One of my old boyfriends lived there. Neither of us had a car so we would take the bus back and forth to hang out and watch the locals play baseball in the summer or ice hockey in the winter.

The Flea Market Tribe
Chapter Ten

"Life and Shopping"

I think it's entirely amazing what people do to earn a living.

I spoke to a man today who has spent his entire life from
the time he was sixteen years of age till now, selling claws,
that came from turtles, bears, squirrels and other
unmentionable animals. He then proceeded to tell me how
he boiled them down in the crockpot.

I was thinking to myself as he amused himself telling me
all this, "What is there no better way to earn a living then to
kill animals and boil their feet in crockpots. And what men
walk around the flea market in a raccoon tail hanging from
his head?"

More needless anxiety led to a stressful day. My elderly
Mother was having surgery, several states away for her
thyroid, which they ended up removing. There was a large
lump that they were sending to pathology.

When I spoke to my husband about this, we ended up
having a very negative conversation, which was not like us.
So for the moment, I felt like the whole world was turned
upside down.

Needing to escape, I decided a good book, a roaring fire,
half a Xanax and early to bed was what the doctor would
order. Some days you need to go to sleep and let the day
end.

Rubbing the sleep from my eyes, I woke up to a much
brighter disposition.

After the car was packed, I was ready to go back to the market.

It seems like the recent break-in was the talk of the town as several people brought it up to me. I told them we should all be vigilant and hope that the police find the culprits.

The day turned out to be a good one with cheerful friends, even though it had rained early and by noon, we all packed up and went home.

With our small quiet town feeling uneasy, I decided to take an unplanned getaway, so I rented a sleeper car.

It is essentially a light towable capsule, that hooks up quite well to my automobile, and I can travel without a hotel. Fundamentally a campground is all I need. I figured with all the chaos going on; it would be good to get out of town for a few days.

I decided to travel to both Vermont and New Hampshire, with the later as my first stop. I wanted to go to out-of-the-way thrift stores, estate sales, and yard sales that I could find.

Sometimes you need to get out of your comfort zone and go on an adventure. It was the first time renting the "towable," and I was certainly enjoying the simplicity of this mode of travel and found the ease of it utterly relaxing.

I was finding some interesting items, including a small collection of Georg Jensen silver. Knowing how collectible it was and that a spoon alone goes for about $140.00 was placing a smile on my face and inside my old body to boot.

Besides, to have matching pieces, not to mention several of them, was unquestionably a great find, which already made the trip worthwhile.

I have been concentrating on purchasing more small items than anything else. Being a minimalist, I don't want to have an over-abundance of clutter even in my selling areas. Clearly, I like to sell items the same week I purchase them as I get bored rather quickly.

I'm also trying to stay away from things that are hard to sell online or not permitted at any of the markets. Such as Coach or Louis Vuitton. If I know that these are authentic, I would rather sell them on Craigslist or let go.

One yard sale that I stopped at had a large selection of bags, plastic, and paper, as well as gift boxes and tissue. Likely this person was a sales rep for the company at one time and was blowing it out. So, I bought a large variety of boxes and bags for ten dollars.

It was a steal, a gifted find, and beyond cool. Something like this ordered from a company would have cost at least a hundred and sixty dollars.

I love to find things that are necessities, whether I can use them at home or in business. That's a real thrill.

As I headed towards Vermont the next day, I began to feel revitalized. I've always enjoyed my trips to Vermont and some of the categorically picturesque little towns.

They have unusual cafés and artsy bookstores. The antique stores and vintage shops are always a worthwhile stop.

While resting in front of the fire pit at the campground, I was watching the live Facebook page of "Sisterhood of the Traveling Trash." And there was a young woman who was a Mother with a few children. Interesting enough, she buys pallets of Kohls and Target clearance merchandise, then hosts a live show on the internet.

So twice a week, she is hawking different merchandise, whether its shoes, health and beauty items or clothing. Sometimes she will be selling jewelry and sunglasses.

It shouldn't surprise me, but it does that I find it so unusual the different ways that people come up with to earn a living. That night, I fell to sleep with that on my mind. As much as I love the flea market, it is taking its toll on me lately.

Waking up, I got an early start as this was my last morning in Vermont. I needed to head back to Maine. The weekend would be here before I knew it and I had a lot of things to set up and prepare.

I had three days of sales ahead of me this weekend, which included an event on Friday that is held quarterly. As an active vendor, you need to arrive at the Trinity church sale at 4:30 in the morning to secure the desired spot. It is also a tremendous place to procure interesting stock, and every time I attend; I keep a very open mind because things are pretty darn inexpensive.

I bought a men's sports bag that I bought for one dollar. Miraculously it sold for over fifty dollars.

I also purchased a Kenneth Jay Lane earring set for five dollars, that sold for forty dollars. Who knew?

Right now Tiki selling is big on the internet. I bought one at a thrift store on this trip to New Hampshire and paid one dollar and fifty cents. When I listed it, with the eBay app on my phone, it had immediate watchers and two bidders.

The travel back home from Vermont was an easy trip, with the weather being so agreeable. All the while, I listened to Journey and Bob Seger, that made the drive fly right by!

By the time I pulled in to my home camp, it was dusk.

I left everything but my travel bags in the car. Everything looked normal and secure at my place. The night was cool, and I started my stove. Then I made some tomato red pepper soup and treated myself to crackers with a little bit of margarine slathered over them.

Pouring into my glass was a cold Lacroix, with a splash of orange juice.

Sipping my soup, I open my latest book, by a new author, Michael Dion. This one was titled "Music is Life and Death. It is his second novel that I have read, and I am enjoying them.

The next day was nice to be able to spend putting things away and getting ready for the three days ahead.

After calling her, it was nice to learn that Lee was going to be attending the Trinity Church sale with me.

After my run-ins with Karen from time to time, I am hesitant occasionally to be going anywhere by myself. It is unusual for me and honestly really pisses me off.

I was angry and didn't want someone else to determine how I made a living or where I could go. So, I was frustrated and needed to figure out how I was going to rectify the situation.

I knew the lady was a drug user. I was sure she was using marijuana, or something else to be under the influence all the time. Subsequently, I contacted Bobby, who then intervened.

The Flea Market Tribe
Chapter Eleven

"The Angry Driver"

I woke up too early for a day off. And even though I have
to get ready for the market, I decided to go to an estate sale.

I left about an hour before the sale started. I always like to
be at least forty-five minutes early. As my husband would
say, "It's a parking thing...".

As I rounded a sharp corner before I could blink an eye, a
black Chevy truck was behind me driving so fast that he
was nearly in my back seat, I thought.

He somehow realized his speed and distance to me, as he
started to brake, and the truck went sideways. Though he
was able to stop his vehicle before smacking into my car,
he was quickly behind me again and honking at me for no
good reason. So I waved my hands to his dismay and
continued to drive the speed limit.

Needless to say that by the time I pulled down the country
lane in the direction of the sale, I was feeling very
unsettled.

Not realizing that he had pulled his truck right behind me in
my parking spot, he stood quickly outside my car as I
exited.

"What are you a tourist?" He yelled.

I was taken back and floored by his rudeness. I had done
nothing wrong, I thought.

He stood there, tall with white hair and tan skin, looking a bit like a Sam Elliot.

"What?" I said to him, as I noticed a banner on his truck from a restaurant one town over.

I then continued, "No, I am not a tourist, but if I were, is that how you want to treat a person who had traveled to see this gorgeous state?"

Wanting to drive home the point, I said to him without fear, "Don't you realize your treatment of others is a calling card for your business?"

Without answering me, he scoffed, grimaced then jumped back in the cab of his truck and was gone before I knew it.

Perhaps he had a tough day already, so I shook off the morning tussle and relaxed as I walked through the rooms of the house, which was a craftsman 1960s style.

I watched the shoppers carry their treasures and couldn't help but wonder why the average shopper was willing to pay eight dollars for something at an estate sale that they wouldn't pay a dollar for at a garage sale. It indeed, does blow my mind.

Strolling back to my car, I left the sale empty handed and went for a drive, to relax.

Ending up at a hospice thrift store, I walked around but wasn't looking for anything. I was sort of unwinding from my scary morning, and besides, I rarely find anything from this store but enjoy checking their shelves and aisles.

I was about to head for the door when I heard that voice.

Of all the places, Karen had just walked through the door!

She did not see me and went about her way asking the salesclerk if they had any new "special" jewelry that had come in and if there was anything put aside for her.

She was apparently looking for any treasure she could score that was unknown to the hospice store staff.

I stayed back turned and faced the men's section. I noticed she talked her way into the back room, and so I made my way out the front door.

I had backed my car into a parking space and noticed that she was parked right beside me. "I wonder if she knew it was me?" I thought.

Looking into her car, I saw that her backseat was filled to the brim. She must have been shopping all day?

Anyway, I drove out of the dirt road lot and didn't stop until I came upon a small fruit stand along the side of the two-lane blacktop. The sign was charming and grabbed my attention..."Just Two Fruits Produce!" Needless to say, the two guys were fabulous!

There I picked up a few things to bring back to my camp and spent the rest of the afternoon in my hammock.

During the early evening, I packed up my car for the adventures ahead. I needed to arrive at the Trinity Church sale at 4:30 sharp in the morning.

At two o'clock in the morning, my phone started ringing off the hook. The unthinkable had happened!

The next day our town had been riveted by something so out of the ordinary, it still rolls around in my head.

The drug cartel supposedly had sent a message. The body of a woman that was frequently seen with Karen was discovered in the lake. She was a very large woman with blond hair. The news report said that she was there for a few days and her body was so bloated that she was almost unrecognizable. The papers did not disclose what Bobby told us in private. "She had an apple stuffed in her mouth and water-proof tape from right below her eyes to the end of her prominent chin."

Whoever did this not only wanted to send a message but also wanted her to experience her final moments? It was clearly being investigated as a homicide, and it wasn't like anything our town had ever seen before.

Everyone at the Trinity church sale was talking about it.

Both Gayle and Lee were there, but we were all extremely busy and dazed by the chaos that had taken over our lives and our little community.

When the ladies and I got together later in the day, we were all stunned and silent, which is not a normal way to describe the three of us.

We all knew Mollie, who was the victim of the lake killing.

None of us were friendly with her, though there were many rumors about her and her family and I try to stay away from as much drama as I can – you know, "not my circus not my monkey!"

As much as I love the market so I'm always wondering if taking off in a motorhome attached to my truck, visiting a different market every week wouldn't suit me better? I would never have to get involved in the drama of others.

Today while packing up my truck, a woman I see around town, yet rarely buys anything, started bending my ear with needless nonsense about politics.

I graciously listen to her for about 15 minutes as the sweat was dripping from my brow.

Finally, I thought to myself, why am I allowing this? It was like she was sucking my soul out through a straw. "Food for thought," I will have to put this on my list of things that I must ponder.

The reality of it all was that at least for the moment, it kind of felt like the devil had taken over our town with things that I never would've imagined were happening. But that's what drugs and crime do, right? There is nothing more or less evil, and we were experiencing it firsthand.

As I gingerly slipped myself into bed, I prayed that things would get better from here on out and that we could figure who was doing all of this.

Meanwhile, on the other side of town, the cartel was making their own plans.

The Flea Market Tribe
Chapter Twelve

"Bobby Burgess"

As a youth in the small Maine town, he longed for the big
city life and the hustle of people and the sounds of life
being lived.

What his real life was, ice hockey on the lake in winter, ice
fishing, and finding lost dogs.

Summer brought tourists, some small-time thieves, lost
purses, more fishing, swimming, canoeing and an
occasional rescue of a child lost in one of the caves.

Some would say that this was stimulating enough, but
Bobby craved excitement and not the kind you get in a
small Maine town.

He had stayed for his Mother Lee, as his father left long
ago.

His Dad's mistress, June was much older than Roger
Burgess but wealthy. Ol' Rog was the kind of guy who
would live off some rich woman in Florida, mainly Key
West.

Much of his time Roger spent on his boat, enjoying lavish
dinners at the club, drinking expensive scotch and not
having to do a day of work.

To say that Bobby had a lot of anger for his father would be
an understatement. He was never there when he was
growing up.

Roger's eyes always had a far-away look, as if he were planning his escape.

Now a portly man with a grey comb-over, his face had become that red blotchy skin from drinking too much.

And while much older than June, he was also blind as a bat.

Most afternoons, he spent at the local massage and bathhouse, where he received an occasional happy ending from Delilah. Inappropriately, Rog with his limited vision, was to sight impaired to realize who Delilah was.

Once famous in her own circle as the grand dame of drag queens, she had not aged well and now was an old transvestite working for tips.

The story of the present day Roger is not who he started out to be. Originally from Massachusetts, he grew up in the established tannery business, working for his father.

Roger had a silver spoon life who never had to work a hard day as everything was presented to him.

Lee, the young girl, and the woman he would eventually marry, came from the wealthy town of Marblehead, Massachusetts. Her family prospered there, with high standings in the social circles and community.

An unusual tight-knit family of four with her younger brother Donald, they all lived a charmed life.

When Lee married Roger, she came to the union with quite a financial bounty. After Lee's parents passed away, she inherited a vast fortune, that unfortunately would be something she would never see again as Roger quickly merged it with his "marital assets" and spent it daily.

Had she been a stronger woman during this time, she could have stopped it, but Roger was slick as they came.

She often wished her father had set the money up as a trust so that she would not have lost control, because when Roger left her, he took her fortune with him.

More than likely, Roger had been hiding money for years, and when he left the bank records showed both he and Lee were broke.

It was a well-known fact and understood that Lee had been robbed by the man she married. He didn't care about if she had money to live on or money to help raise their son.

Lee was left alone needing funds to survive on and never had enough to hire an attorney to try and get her assets back. It was a lost cause in the end.

Faced with a dire dilemma, she eventually took to refinishing furniture and "upcycling" items to sell at the flea market. It occurred because a friend in town needed some help in his shop and paid her cash along with furniture that people never returned to pick up.

Living like this, it afforded Lee the opportunity to be home a great deal with her son during the week.

Lee devoted her life to Bobby. She knew that he did not ask to be born. Even so, she and Roger chose to bring him into the world. So now as his Mother and a darn good one as people would tell her, she was going to put her child first, every single time.

This devotion meant a lot to Bobby, who wanted to be a different kind of man. His father, in his mind, was a dirtbag having left him and his Mother.

Bobby had grown up closely with Peyton, who was Jillian's son. They went through school together and played sports and would likely be just as close if Peyton had not moved away. He was sincerely happy for his old friend who was now married with four-year-old twin boys.

But Bobby had not settled down, though there had been several serious relationships. Besides police work and caring for his Mom, it left little time for marriage, or a reason to leave Maine.

As far as he was concerned, since his Mother had raised him all on her own, she now deserved the luxury of having her only child be loyal to her and live in the same town.

His Mother and the other Tribe member of gals were always threatening to set him up with Gayle's daughter Eden, who was a lovely English girl.

They all repeated their efforts in tandem conversations with him whenever they had a chance. But Bobby would smile and wave them off as he thought it was too close for comfort with the "old Hens." (As he referred to his Mother and her friends lovingly).

Besides any relationship, this close to home could get himself in trouble, and though somewhere inside him he wished he had settled down and found a partner for life, as Peyton had, he was a little too fearful of finding out.

For the moment, Bobby needed to get back to his real life and the crime syndicate that had infiltrated his town. The last thing Bobby ever expected was a gruesome murder!

He thought that the break-ins and drugs were shocking enough, but this was blowing his mind.

The "Big City Life" had come to haunt him and his sleepy small artsy town. That lore of excitement and drama had certainly presented itself, but not in the way he had hoped.

The Flea Market Tribe
Chapter Thirteen

"Lovely Eden"

Eden Collins was a shy and demure young woman with
sandy blonde hair, a delicate nose that kind of turned up at
the end. Her hazel eyes were bewitching, and she had
beautiful hands with long fingers. Her grandmother always
called them "piano hands."

Living in a small town called Bridgnorth, it was part of the
beautiful green English Countryside in the rural county of
Shropshire. The town was split into two parts across the
River Severn. The northern section on one side and the
southern side on the other. The population only had two
thousand people, and that was during the tourist season.

She had been helping her Mother and Aunt run The Cottage
Tea Room from the time that she was a young girl. She
started behind the scenes, helping to prepare the classic
four tea sandwiches: cucumber, egg salad, chicken with
cranberry and their famous smoked salmon along with the
traditional selection of biscuits and cookies.

As she grew her up, her responsibilities multiplied. It
included buying local wares from the town folk that sold in
the summer to both tourist and locals alike.

Her Mother Gayle was quite savvy by selling the stocked
local soap company products. She knew how to market
them and would insert these into the privy to give the
customer a real-life countryside experience. It always paid
for itself, with a profit margin of almost 1000%. Her
personal favorite was the date and fig bar that she shared
with her customers.

Another part of their shop sold antiquities that Gayle had procured throughout the decades.

As time went on and her Aunt Dorothy retired, Eden took over the books, since she had graduated from the local University and was keen with numbers.

With Eden's father long gone, her Mother, Gayle began to travel more frequently to America. She had fallen in love with the state of Maine after a visit to her pen pal Lee.

Gayle started by spending summers in an air stream on Lee's property, but once Gayle made the move to the States full time, she purchased her own camp.

With the relocation of her Mother, Eden took over the Tea Room full time. Though the town was small, the business was right next to the Charity Shop and was a definite draw, particularly during the spring, summer and fall months.

Eden had grown up frugally and found all of her special clothing pieces right next door, especially after watching a documentary on YouTube that changed her life on minimalism. It tied nicely into managing the Tea Shop and her personal lifestyle.

Eden was the kind of gal that was so naturally beautiful inside and out that people were always drawn to her. Nevertheless, men were always threatened by her. Perhaps it was because she was so headstrong.

Since her Mother moved to the United States, she had purchased her own cottage, which was located in the back of the Tea Room. She loved having the simplicity that surrounded her every day as it was decorated sparsely, yet even in the coldest days, it still warmed her inside and out.

After speaking with her Mum about the recent break-in of her house, she planned a trip to see her. Eden wanted to check on her following the incident, but having never visited America, she was nervous but looked forward to this new adventure and place that her Mother so loved.

Eden had to go to the local post office to apply for her passport. She knew it would take a couple of weeks, so she waited patiently for the mail before booking her trip.

Gayle meanwhile was dealing with a horrific situation in her town, and everyone was clearly on edge.

The day at the Trinity church sale was not a sales success due to a small turnout because of the Lake Murder.

Many of the locals didn't want to leave home, and the rest just wanted to find out more information. Gayle had two days of the Flea Market ahead and still had the truck packed and ready to go.

She thought that when her home was broken into and, the stolen ring ended up at the market on the table of Thomas was crazy enough. However, a town that rarely had any crime was now dealing with its first murder in twenty-two years was more than anyone could imagine.

Coming from such a quiet place in the English countryside with its gentle life, this was playing havoc with Gayle's digestive system. She was constantly running for the privy, thank goodness her booth at the flea market was directly facing one. Still, that is not something that you can schedule.

Days like these, she realized how blessed she was to have her sisters by choice, her tribe so closely by her side.

Coupled with Lee, they shared a long history of being pen pals first. It was followed by renting her travel trailer and living on her property in those early days of Gayle's American journey.

Meeting Jillian was a real treat that she didn't expect. From the moment they met, it was as if they knew each other. They both shared the same sense of humor and could crack the other up with just a smirk.

Jillian had helped her procure the items for her camp, which paid homage to her English upbringing. Eden would often send her things that were light in shipping weight, and she loved getting care packages from her daughter.

The gal pals were always saying that they needed to introduce Eden to Bobby. Not because they were both single but because they were some of their most favorite people. Though to look at them, they couldn't have been more different, except in looks, because they were both extremely attractive.

However, Eden was well read, maybe not as educated in the world as Bobby, but Eden had very few suitors in her lifetime.

Bobby, on the other hand, was more of a short relationship kind of guy. The girls that dated Bobby knew that he was not the marrying kind. But he was special, and you knew that just being in his presence. He was the all American with good looks, spectacular vocabulary, chiseled physic from athletic training, and all around good guy.

Bobby often wished he could just let go and open himself up to the idea of a relationship. Always in the back of his mind was the idea of someday being a dad, a kind of father he'd always wanted. The kind that would be true to his wife. A father that his children could trust. A son to play ice hockey with or a daughter to braid her hair. These were constantly there in his mind, but then reality would strike back, and his heart would pull up the familiar walls.

"Sometimes they seemed like they were log and sometimes shiplap," Bobby thought to himself.

When the station called, he was off, jumping into his Ford F-150 Raptor with huge wheels and a heavy duty tow bar.

The crime syndicate had made another move.

The Flea Market Tribe
Chapter Fourteen

"Crime Gone Wild"

Karen was hiding out with her husband. The trailer park on the edge of town was the kind of place one could get lost for a while.

After Mollie's grotesque murder, Karen knew the "message" was directed at her. What started as a small time operation had not only gotten out of control but had her frightened beyond anything she could ever imagine. She wanted out.

She wondered if Thomas and the refinery guy were feeling the heat?

The brothers that Karen was doing business with came by her trailer that evening unexpected. They had gold to trade for drugs. These guys were into oxi and zanies (street slang).

After Karen weighed out the gold for her husband, they traded out the gold for money but eyed the brothers cautiously.

The brothers made mention of Mollie's murder and said their boss was getting a push elsewhere to bring their business to the other side of town.

This only made Karen that much nervous and wasn't looking forward to scraping up car payments but being broke outweighed being dead any day.

On the south side of town where the two motels were located, Johnny "are we having fun yet" Burton had his crew planning a visit to some of his competition.

The quiet town that was a mix of retirees, locals, and tourists was just his home base, though his operation actually encompassed many counties. His research into the small town with barely a police department was not going to be much trouble for Johnny B.

As a businessman, Johnny was originally from Boston, where he spent his summers on Cape Cod bartending at the Brothers Four on the beach. He had lived in one of the cottages the hotel rented out to their staff.

Johnny always had a bounty of beautiful women on his arm. He didn't normally mess with the local girls as they caught on too easy, but there were a few that made it past his bravado.

Back at the flea market, Jillian spent the next two days as things seemed to be quite calm. The weather was gorgeous, and it brought everyone out, young and old.

Monday morning came, and as she went into town to pick up a few things and go to the post office, she climbed the few steps to the post office and reached for the door.

There a man walked out that held the door open for her. She thanked the tall stranger who seemed familiar to her, by the cologne that he wore. She was nearly inside the door when she heard his voice…"Jilly?"

"Jillian Dione is that you?"

A million things raced through her head. "Nope. Not me. Wrong girl."

Girl...she was merely a woman when she met Johnny B that first summer on the Cape.

She turned to face him as he was standing right in front of her after climbing up the two steps to greet her.

"Yes, that is me!"

"Well, don't you remember me?" he said with a huge smile.

"Johnny B…Cape Cod, Brothers' 4, Falmouth Heights Beach .... you and me?"

"Some of those details are familiar," Jillian replied.

"Did you also have an older brother?" she continued.

"Why yes, I do, but you're just playing coy with me Missy, I know you gotta remember me?"

"What are you doing here in Maine?" Johnny asked.

"I've spent most of my life here. Raised a family," Jillian replied.

"Give me your number," Johnny said. "I'm new to this town. I'll take you to dinner. You can show me around."

"Sorry, Johnny," Jillian replied. "My husband doesn't let me out on dates unless they outrank him. You're not by chance a Rear Admiral, are you?"

"Very funny Jilly... where are you working these days?"

She told him, and that was likely a mistake.

Later that day on her hammock, she let her mind wander back to being that naive girl she once was.

She had met Johnny B at the Captain Kidd restaurant and bar in Woods Hole. She was waitressing, and a group of guys and gals took over one of her tables. He was a tall impressive young man, introducing himself as Johnny B. He told her that he was bartending at Brothers' 4 that had some signature drinks that he wanted to make me, "A slippery nipple" being one of them.

My first thought was, "Another crude SOB," but he was dead serious.

In a shot glass, he poured Rumple-mints, floated Kailua, and finished by floating Baileys Irish Cream.

The group was a loud yet fun bunch, and in the end, I was tipped handsomely for my hard work and attention to detail.

Johnny B thanked me and said, "Don't forget tomorrow is ladies' night at Brothers Four. You should come by! I will be at Bar B; you know for Johnny B".

The next night I learned where the "Are we having fun yet" came from.

He was a showman behind the bar.

A few more nights later, he came into Captain Kidd and asked me on a date.

I said, "Yes, only because you make me laugh."

On that night, he picked me up, and after a quiet bite, took me to Brothers Four. He seemed very attentive. Whenever he would leave to speak to someone or use the restroom, he would always tell one of his buddies, "Keep an eye on her."

In my naive young state, I thought that meant I was special to him, like a fine sculpture or painting that needed to be guarded. I should have known better.

It took me a while to figure out that keeping an eye on Johnny's date was only to protect him from anyone discovering what he later claimed were simply shenanigans.

I soon tired of his kind of fun and finally figured out who he really was, or so I thought then.

Now thirty-five years later, Jillian still remembered.

Back at the hotel, Johnny B was floored to have run into Jilly. He had dated her on and off on the Cape three decades ago.

Back in the early days, his father would send his two sons to the Cape for the summers. Some of those friendships had lasted a lifetime, and some of those friends took a vested interest in his success became lieutenants in the organization.

In his office, Johnny settled into his leather desk chair and couldn't help but smirk.

"Jillian Dione. Quite interesting," he said to himself out loud.

Johnny didn't like romantic situations. It complicated his business affairs. Yet, Jilly was definitely one gal that pulled no punches back in the day. Though naive in love or sexual encounters, she was sharp as a knife when it came to life. She was a memory he carried because she totally blew him off once she figured him out. Something none of the other "chickies" did. Every broad except Jilly thought they could change him.

Jillian had a spark. It was something the three Dione sisters shared. They had something that made you want to know more about them.

There was a saying amongst the sisters. "Can't fight that DS-The Dione Spark!"

Johnny remembered the middle sister coming into the Brothers Bar with a fake id. He always gave her a pass, as to not piss off her older sister.

When Jillian was working at Captain Kidd, she was notorious for checking the faces in her sister's high school yearbook so that she could confiscate fake IDs.

The ATF (Alcohol Tobacco and Firearms) on the Cape, were known to pay bartenders $25.00 per confiscated fake drivers' license.

Jillian had always been an entrepreneur and made legitimate side money wherever she could.

The Flea Market Tribe
Chapter Fifteen

"White Pine Ridge"

Elaina and Jose Castro were sound asleep, in the guest cottage on the property owned by their youngest daughter Miranda.

The night was still at White Pine Ridge when Jose was woken abruptly from the sound of glass breaking.

Jose told his wife to be silent.

He grabbed his Glock G17 and made his way out the door and crept along the hallway. As he came around the corner, he found two jokers carrying electronics and a backpack heading outside the front door.

The back door was wide open, so they looked like they were not done with robbery.

Jose waited along the wall to make sure there were only two guys.

As the two robbers returned from the car, Jose, who had just called 911 stepped out of the darkness and shouted stop and get on the floor.

The larger guy of the two removed his sidearm and fired at Jose. Jose fired back, hitting the robber's leg. The two then ran off as the red droplets fell on the ground leaving a path.

As Jose checked himself, to make sure he hadn't been hit, Elaina was screaming from inside the cottage.

The sirens shrieked, and then stopped as police fanned out at the cottage. Jose praised God, not only had he and his wife survived, but he was not hit by the gunfire at all.

Bobby and his team arrived like a swarm of bees.

Outside standing by the police cars, the Castro's were shaken by the robbery as they spoke with the first officer on the scene.

They were making a statement for the record. The two were still trembling. Mr. Castro more so, as he had never fired his gun at someone before much less hit them.

The Castro's were not supposed to be there that night, but their daughter Miranda was out of town for business with her husband. And they wanted to go to the flea market the next day.

The family, including Miranda and her husband, owned a small two-store chain of jewelry stores, mainly specializing in Jose Castro's gold designs.

Once the house was secure, the Castro's checked into the motel for the night. After Jose and his wife Elaina unpacked their overnight bags, Jose asked his wife if he should contact his attorney even though the Police said it was not necessary.

Jose had done everything by the book, including coming to America from his beloved Portugal. His first job was in Philadelphia working at the meat packing plant. He needed a steady income if he and Elaina were to start a family, and jewelry design would have to take a back seat to a weekly paycheck.

As he snuggled his wife of 35 years, he choked back his tears. He had done everything to stay within the law, and now he had shot a man.

Bobby called his Mother. "Mom, I want you and the girls to know there was another break-in tonight at White Pine Ridge."

Bobby then went on to tell her the story about the activities that happened that night. He didn't want her to be blindsided by the news in the morning or by the many storytellers at the flea market.

Lee never went back to sleep that night, knowing that the two criminals were still on the loose.

Bobby had told her that they had recovered DNA at the scene that stemmed from the blood found which probably came from one of the robbers that Jose shot.

Lee called both Jillian and Gayle to tell them both what had happened during the night.

Gayle told her that she would bring coffee and biscuits in the morning and to meet in our row before setting up for the day.

That morning, sitting on top of the wooden tables that were permanent fixtures at the market, drinking coffee and eating Gayle's homemade delicacies we couldn't help but wonder where was this all going?

Jillian brought everyone up to speed on the story about Johnny B.

Lee then relayed Bobby's story about attending the funeral of Mollie on police business, of course.

Mollie's son told stories about growing up with his Mother and missing the cackle of her laugh.

I thought that was a mean thing to say as I surely would not miss it. That woman had disgusted me for years. But this was not a nice thing to say since we all have our issues, peculiar habits and who knows what. I then told myself to be nice. You never know anyone and what they have gone through in life.

Gayle, on the other hand, was full of positive news as she was looking forward to her daughter booking her trip to the United States. She had not seen her for two years straight, even though they spoke often, wrote letters, and emailed each other to stay in touch.

That day the market was booming. The sunshine created a beautiful day that brought everyone out. The retirees must've received their social security checks because they were spending it for once. For just a moment, it seemed like old times before all of this other craziness in town.

Bobby had told Lee that they were waiting for the DNA results from the lab as they were certain this character must be in the system. We were hopeful to remove one more loser off the street.

Missing from the market, Karen had received word that one of her associates had been injured in the robbery that occurred up on White Pine Ridge. It was not one of her main guys but someone that she made purchases from or traded with.

Karen was extremely nervous, feeling like the robberies were getting too close to her.

She tried to convince her husband it was time to bail out, but he refused since he was addicted and able to pay for his habit by his selling and trading the drugs

Getting older by the moment, Karen walked into an estate sale with a cigarette squeezed between her thin lips. Her female mustache had become yellow from the tar and nicotine. And her eyes were framed with lines from squinting through cheap Dollar Store readers.

Leaving the estate sale with a box of vintage jewelry, she rounded the corner to place everything in her car. But she found Bobby Burgess from the Sheriff's Department sitting on top of it.

"Yeah, what's up?" She asked him.

"Well, ma'am," said Bobby, "Looks to me like your plates are out of date."

She said to him with a smart ass grin, "Yeah." I sent in for them, but this damn state drags their feet on everything. What is it about us common working folks? You're always riding our ass."

"Look," Bobby said. "I was more than professional with you. And considering you've got a rap sheet two miles long, you might not want to be such a Smart Alec. Speaking of that, what do you know about the break-in on White Pine Ridge a few nights ago?"

Bobby went on, "The rumor is that you might know something about who we've been looking for?"

Karen surprised by the statement and now nervous replied. "Talk to my lawyer as I've got nothing to do with that." "Sure?" Bobby sarcastically said. Then he wrote her a ticket for expired plates.

Pissed, Karen crumpled up the ticket and threw it on the ground before he even pulled out of the lot.

The Flea Market Tribe
Chapter Sixteen

"Selling Gold"

Jillian settled into her living room area after a long day at the market.

"A chill in the night? Or was my soul feeling the unrest?", she thought to herself, lighting her pellet stove.

She had felt like she had all the pieces to the puzzle that encircled the town, but that she wasn't putting them in the correct order:

1. Karen had an endless supply of gold. Where was she really getting it from?
2. How did Mollie's death tie into it all?
3. Thomas, who was buying all of Karen's gold, was acting desperate.
4. Blaine was present, but something was definitely up with him.
5. Drugs had invaded the small town. Where were they coming from?
6. Homes were getting robbed? This from a town that was basically crime free?
7. A suspect was shot by a homeowner's family member.

Then it dawned on Jillian! Karen was involved in all of this. Or was it her dislike of Karen, or was she seriously all over these events?

Was it that simple? Because it felt like something much bigger.

I needed to do some more investigating.

On the second day of the flea market, I decided to do some shopping.

A vintage sewing basket cost me three dollars, and two bottles of perfume rang up for a total of five dollars.

A pair of sterling silver earrings that were so amazing for one dollar, that I chuckled to myself, saying, "I may need to keep them."

The other items totaled only eight dollars to purchase but resulted in sales of seventy dollars. Perfume always sells, so it ended up being a stellar day.

As for the vintage sewing basket, I always keep a few ten cent garage sale finds in a box, that will sell along with other vintage notions placed in the basket which will up the value every time and ultimately reap a pretty penny.

As the market opened, I watched Karen walk over to Thomas. She was tight-lipped. They didn't have a lot to say to each other, nor did they exchange pleasantries.

He weighed the gold, and Karen supervised Thomas because she had already weighed it herself and knew what it should amount to. He paid her, and she left. It was very professional, maybe too much so. It was unlike any other time they traded.

Within an hour, Karen's husband arrived at the market, and I watched him take something out of her trunk and put it into his cross body messenger bag. Then he and his guy pal walked to the other side of the market.

Blaine casually walked to Thomas's booth and bought the scrape that he had for the refinery.

Then I watched as Blaine purchased a second bag from Thomas, which was a completely different transaction.

Bewildered, the question remained, "Why was Karen not selling her gold directly to Blaine? I knew I was on to something.

While walking up and down the aisle during the slow times, I used this to get my steps in. I do try for at least 6000 per day.

One of the vendors Jeff stopped me and started a conversation.

He is a middle-aged man with shoulder-length hair. I wasn't too sure what his situation was as he seemed a little bit feminine to me. Though it didn't matter to me since I have been an ally for the LGBT community all of my life.

He asked me if I had seen Blaine today? I told him that I saw him earlier with Thomas.

He then asked me if I had sold gold to either of them?

I told him that I had to both of them in the past.

I then stated, "I don't understand why Karen would sell her goal to Thomas rather than Blaine since Thomas was the middleman."

Jeff replied, "Oh, Blaine is way too smart to buy that gold firsthand."

I said, "What?"

I tried to ask him what he meant, but a customer had popped up and took his attention away.

When I returned to my booth, I sat "crisscross applesauce" on one of the extra tables. My sisters and I would play games sitting with our legs crossed and would always sing out that phrase.

However, within an hour, Jeff walked straight up to me and whispered in my ear and said one word, "drugs."

Backing away, he quietly told me, "Blaine gives me $150.00 a month to keep my mouth shut."

However, with my mouth now wide open, Jeff started to walk away, and I blurted out, "Wait!"

He looked back around and said, "What now? Are you writing a book?"

"Maybe I should be," I replied.

Wanting to know more, I asked him, "If Blaine is paying you $150.00 a month to keep your mouth shut, why are you telling me?"

He shrugged his shoulders and walked away.

Befuddled, I thought to myself, "Did he just help me? Or was he sending me on a wild goose chase for a reason? And lastly, should I be writing a book?" as Jillian chuckled to herself.

The market ended calmly, and I returned home.

Following a long night of tossing and turning, I went to see Bobby at the station. There wasn't one thing that kept me from sleeping. It just was a rough night, with thoughts of everything floating around my brain.

When I arrived, Bobby was in his office and waved me in.

Jillian genuinely knew that if she weren't one of his Mother's best friends, she would not be receiving this sort of welcome. Bobby Burgess was a busy man these days

So without hesitation, I laid it all out for him. Everything that I could think of and from where I'd gotten my information.

Rather than poo-poo me, Bobby said that I had some valid points and that he would check into them. He also divulged that they had received the DNA results from the blood of Jimmy Smith, who was also known as Smitty.

Jimmy "Smitty" was a local break-in & entry guy that was well known for trying to feed his habit. The cops were keeping an eye out for him but wanted me to know that his prior associates included Karen and her husband. Unfortunately, it also included Mollie and that he had a romantic past with her.

Bobby said goodbye and was soon making his way through town. The cops had placed an APB out for Smitty, but he hadn't shown up anywhere yet.

That night, Bobby pulled into his Mother's driveway to give her an update on the latest, and as I found out later, he also related to Lee what I had told him earlier in the day.

As Bobby told his Mom the information, Lee made her almost-famous peanut butter and jelly sandwich. In fact, at a town social one year, she made everyone her special sandwich. It was later learned that she sprinkled cinnamon and nutmeg into the peanut butter which added that incredible tang. It was probably the best on the planet.

Though a bit childish, Lee took great pleasure out of making this for her son, as much as Bobby enjoyed it.

The Flea Market Tribe
Chapter Seventeen

"Blaine"

As he made his way over to the refinery, he felt an
argument coming on. His business partner Frank was way
more difficult these days.

The flea market had always been a stupendous outlet for
buying precious metals. The one thing that Frank lacked
was s code of ethics.

Blaine was careful. He used Thomas as the middleman
whenever buying the metal, so he was not associating with
questionable or known criminals, as his attorney had
advised him.

He knew that Thomas had been sucked into this long ago
when the payout to Karen was more cash than he could
come up with.

So Thomas approached Blaine for the cash.

In the beginning, he still got a nice return of the investment,
But the more he dealt with Karen and others, the less he
received back, after paying for the money.

Thomas realized that the further he went down this "rabbit
hole," the easier it was for Blaine to blackmail him.
Regrettably, he was doing the trading to keep his head
above water and his body out of the landfill.

Now entering his office building, Blaine headed for his
office.

The two partners offices were separated by a common area, with extra seating, a kitchen, and the restroom.

Frank was from a well to do New England family and was a very private man.

Blaine knew almost nothing about his personal life. He wasn't married and associated with less than a handful of people that Blaine had met. Some would consider it secrecy, but Blaine thought it was because he didn't have any friends since he never mentioned what he did on the weekends, or outside of work.

Blaine waved at Frank as Blaine entered his own office. Frank exchanged the pleasantries.

Blaine looked at himself in the mirror that hung above the leather sofa. The worry and the stress were causing him to go prematurely gray. The frown lines were obvious, and his warm Armenian skin tone was looking pale.

If he didn't have so many balls in the air, he would treat himself to a vacation somewhere warm and sunny with several cocktails and a few local island girls to take his mind off his troubles at home.

But he had a business to take care of, and he was clearly getting frustrated that though he was taking all of the chances with the gold purchases, Frank seemed to be reaping most of the benefits.

Blaine was trying to figure a way to bury some of the profits from Frank. He didn't like the idea of the dirty business, so maybe he thought he should input "operation scrub," after all these years.

It's not that Frank did anything other than work in his office, or Blaine thought. On most nights, Frank could be found there as late as 10 pm.

Frank lived in a small, nondescript condominium, just outside the town square and drove a Toyota Camry sedan, which was not the least bit flashy.

But before Blaine could think more about what to do, Frank entered his office.

"Blaine, I have been going over the books," Frank blurted out.

As he continued, he said, "Something looks really funky to me. Now I'm no forensic accountant, but I certainly could find one. Why are you withdrawing large sums of cash?"

Blaine replied, "Frank, we've been over this. This is the way we purchase gold and jewelry from outside vendors."

Blaine was plainly frustrated and told Frank, "As long as the numbers lineup, in the end, don't worry about it!"

At home, Jillian woke up early for a non-market day.

Sitting in her vintage styled kitchen, she read the local paper. There had been no break-ins since the Castro shooting and the police were still searching for their suspect, Jimmy.

After doing her chores, she headed out to the garden. It was a success this year, and the bounty was delicious!

Jillian was overjoyed as she picked some extra fruit and veggies to bring to Lee and Gayle when they met for lunch at noon. While still in the garden, a young man walked around back.

Jillian was scared since she rarely had unannounced visitors.

"Miss Jillian?"

"Yes," I replied. "How can I help you?" standing up, brushing sod off my apron.

He stated that he had a delivery for me, and in a flash, he was gone to fetch it.

When he returned, he was holding the most beautiful bouquet of Calla Lilies, that I had ever seen.

Since my husband was traveling, I thought they must be from him. But as I removed the card, I smelled a very familiar scent, and the note inside confirmed my suspicion.

The card read:
"I had missed that face.
J.B."

"Johnny Burton?"

At first, I wondered how he could have known my address but soon realized that my name was on file at the local shop, "Sugar Maple Florist."

Part of me was a little giddy girl loving the attention but then realized this was definitely not a good thing.

After deciding not to throw them away, because the bouquet was vast, I split them in three to share with the girls along with my garden offerings.

When I met up with them later, I relayed the situation. Gayle loved the treats, but Lee said, you know, "Calla Lilies are funeral flowers!"

"That may be," I told Lee. "But where I grew up calla lilies lined our side fence, facing bottle brush on the other side. Johnny B must have remembered that these were my favorite flowers."

We had not been sitting there for more than 10 minutes before Johnny B walked into the dinner.

Walking directly over to our table, he greeted me with a kiss on my cheek.

"I see you got the flowers," Johnny said. "But you're giving them away?"

I replied, "No, Johnny, you sent three dozen, and I figured I could share."

I then introduced the ladies to Johnny, and as they reached out their hands to greet him, he kissed each one.

Gayle said, "Wow, you are quite a gentleman."

Lee said, "You know these flowers are for funerals, right?"

Johnny looked surprised and glanced at me.

I looked back and shook my head at him and said, "Apparently, my friend. has a one-track mind when it comes to these flowers."

Not responding but smiled slyly, Johnny exchanged pleasantries as he left and sat in a booth by the window.

Lee said, "So what's his deal? What's he doing here?"

I told them all I knew, and what he told her. "He was here in town to invest in some property for his family."

Gayle said, "He's sort of a polished dude."

Then Lee said, "Way too polished if you know what I mean!"

As I excused myself to go to the restroom, I washed my hands, and as I dried them, I couldn't help but notice that they were looking more like my Mother's hands every day.

Leaving the bathroom, I encountered Johnny on my way out.

"Jilly, my dear Jilly! I have been invited to the summer home of the Governor of this great state. Please tell me you will attend this invite with me. New in town, I hardly know a soul."

"John," I Said. "I am married and cannot attend this with you or anything else. It would not be right."

"Jillian," he replied with that sheepish grin, "I am asking you purely out of friendship.

Smiling back at him, I asked, "Were the flowers out of friendship as well?"

"Well, yes," he said.

"Imagine," I thought to myself, "My delight to encounter a friend I haven't seen in so many years, to still be that smooth. It really piqued my curiosity for sure. So I gave him my card and told him, "I would think about it."

The Flea Market Tribe
Chapter Eighteen

"Smitty"

I returned to the table to a beaming Gayle! Eden was coming to Maine!

She was on FaceTime with Eden, and we all took turns passing the phone around.

We were all so preoccupied; we did not see Bobby standing there, as Lee passed the phone back to Gayle,

Then Lee looked up and saw Bobby.

Lee yelled out, "Wait," and grabbed the phone back from Gayle. Looking into the phone, Lee said, "Eden, please meet my son Bobby."

Bobby just stood there with the phone in his hand as his cheeks flushed red with embarrassment.

The young woman raised her head to meet Bobby's gaze.

"Well, hello there," Eden said with her beautiful accent and dancing eyes.

"You must be Bobby! Guess that makes me, Eden," she continued.

Bobby laughed at her cheerful introduction.

"I understand you are coming for your first trip to Maine?" Bobby stated.

Eden responded, "Yes though I'm a smidge nervous since my Mum had told me about the goings-on in town."

I can assure you, Miss Eden, we all will look after you.

Later that day, Eden still felt the warmth on her cheeks from the impromptu meeting with Bobby via FaceTime.

She had heard a lot about him over the last few years but had never even seen a photograph. He had sandy blonde hair and a boyish grin that made his eyes light up. And she heard a man with a hearty yet sweet laugh.

Quickly this trip was becoming more exciting, she thought. Smiling to herself, the young tea room owner prepped the egg salad for the following day.

As Bobby entered the station after lunch, he really couldn't get the FaceTime call with Eden out of his mind. She was certainly lovely, but her relation to Gayle was a little too close.

Though his aunts by choice, Gayle and Jillian had never been pushy with his personal life, his dear Mother was another story altogether.

All of these thoughts rolling around in his head were cut short by a frantic call from one of the sisters that owned the small motels on the edge of town.

"Possible 187, homicide.

Bobby and his team rushed out to the scene. They came in through the lounge area of the motel through the pool area, where several senior citizens were sitting in pool chairs.

His training kicked in. Number one, "Access the situation."

The group of seniors taking their weekly water yoga class had noticed a pool lounge chair at the bottom of the pool.

They left it alone until the motel staff could get a busboy to go in with swim trunks so he could retrieve it.

Once the young man Clyde went in the pool, he tried to move the chair, and an arm popped out the side.

Clyde swam to the top as if he'd seen a shark and told the people standing around to call 911.

Next to respond was the fire department, and Bobby asked them to retrieve the lounge chair.

Though he was unrecognizable with the plastic bag around his head, the wound on his leg confirmed to Bobby that they had just found Jimmy Smith.

As the small forensic team showed up, the police finished all the interviews and Bobby headed off to the station.

On his way, he called his Mother to let her know what had transpired and that Jimmy Smith was no longer on the street, but he was on a slab in the morgue.

After completing the paperwork and hitting the gym in a space underneath the police station, Bobby showered and headed out. He decided to go back to the crime scene at the motel to see if there was anyone there who saw anything else regarding the murder.

As he pulled up, he saw a banner, "Appearing nightly:

Chained Lightning, come on in, their knocking them dead!"

Strolling into the lounge area, Bobby saw the plexiglass sign holders that spelled out the drink special. "Bottom of the pool: a snifter of Sambuca with a coffee bean floating in it."

Bobby thought, "Their marketing department was certainly crass."

With nothing new to help him in the murder, he headed home with his thoughts turning to Eden and her upcoming visit.

The next two days flew by. And though the cops knew that Jimmy Smith had been murdered, they did not have a suspect. The medical examiner did confirm that he died by strangulation and it had nothing to do with his earlier gunshot.

The medical examiner was able to confirm that his leg had been treated by a medical clinic or personnel.

Lee called both Gayle and Jillian. She told them that the police were now dealing with the second murder in their small town.

That evening, I called Bobby at home.

"Hi Jillian," he answered.

"I'm just checking back. I wanted to know if you had gone over all the information that I brought you? The timeline? The chain of events? And who do you think killed Jimmy Smith?"

"Jillian, I will be in the office bright and early. I don't like to talk about it through the landlines. So come in, let's talk, and bring some bagels."

As I hung up, I thought to myself, "Once a boy always a boy."

I knew I was avoiding the real issue, Johnny B! After giving him my number, I wondered if he would call? I was certain that going to this shindig with him would be wrong and that my husband wouldn't approve. However, I was curious, "What was he really doing here of all places?"

I thought, "Am I fooling myself, was I lonely and didn't want to admit that?"

Johnny B and I had a past, yet I think inside I always felt he stole my innocence from me.

Sitting at the bar at Delmonico's, Johnny was drinking wine. The bar was just inside the town square, where Johnny heard the patrons discussing the murder of that "scum-bucket" Jimmy Smith. Outwardly, it had the locals in a twist.

Johnny smiled like a Cheshire cat as he looked inside the glass, then after taking another sip, smiled again.

The Flea Market Tribe
Chapter Nineteen

"The Moment with Eden"

Eden's arrival had everyone excited.

Her Mother drove to Bangor to meet her plane connecting from New York.

She arrived wearing a lovely summer dress, white cotton with yellow sunflowers. She reminded Gayle of her younger self.

"We've been invited for a quiet dinner at Lee's house if you're up for it?", Gayle told her daughter.

"You mean dinner with Bobby? Right, Mum?' laughingly replied, Eden.

"Well, I am sure he will be there," Gayle said. But to herself, she thought Bobby might be too busy with the most recent murder.

They had a several hour drive to get home, and Mother and Daughter chatted like schoolgirls.

Gayle was thrilled and couldn't wait to take Eden to the flea market and share her with her many friends.

When they finally arrived at Lee's house, she noticed Bobby's truck and smiled.

"Oh look, Eden," Gayle said, "Bobby is already here!"

Though Eden tried to freshen up at the rest stop, she had just flown eight hours and regrettably, she thought, she looked like it.

As Eden slipped out of the car, another truck pulled up, and soon Eden was being hugged by Jillian as the three women were laughing and embracing each other.

Bobby was watching out the cabin window and immediately said, "Eden and the tribe have arrived Mom. She is much more prettier than I expected."

Lee smiled as she came scurrying into the room while removing her apron.

All Bobby could think to himself was, "This lovely English woman could be trouble."

The three ladies walked through the front door, and soon there were four hens clucking thought Bobby.

As Eden emerged from the nest, she walked over and said with her hand stretched out, "Lovely to meet you, Bobby."

For a moment, even after the long flight, he thought to himself, a young Audrey Hepburn.

Bobby was fumbling a little but took her hand and kissed the top of her beautiful long fingers. He could feel a spark that started at his lips, which ended in his toes, he was sure of it.

As he gazed at Eden, still holding her hand, time seemed to stand still, and then the moment was lost as Lee started barking orders at everyone.

The group of us then moved to the dining room, sat down, and Bobby started pouring the champagne and passed the glasses to each of the women, except to Jillian.

Besides her, the other one not indulging was Bobby since he was on call. The two then drank club soda, and the rest of the group all understood and respected Jillian's sobriety.

Bobby seemed to be one of those dinners that didn't get a word in edgewise since there was much laughing, drinking, and storytelling. But he was fine with that, besides he kept looking at Eden and she at him.

When the evening was over, Bobby offered to drive Gayle and Eden home. He figured that they could pick up their car in the morning.

But Gayle thanked him and said they'd already accepted Jillian's offer for a ride.

"No problem," Bobby said.

Everyone hugged each other goodbye. Then the three ladies were off.

Bobby couldn't help but smile. He could still smell her light floral fragrance from the hug goodbye and the soft kiss on his cheek.

Eden woke more than a few times that night with the time difference, and certainly, the sparkling wine didn't help much.

Knowing that her Mother always set the coffee up tonight before she snuck into the kitchen and found her sitting there at the table.

"Mum, I know you're an early riser, but what are you doing up so early?" asked Eden.

"Planning my grandchildren," Gayle answered with a grin on her face.

The Flea Market Tribe
Chapter Twenty

"Karen"

To say that Karen was scared was an understatement.

Before Mollie's death, she was giving Karen strange vibes and saying outlandish things.

Karen wished she could remember everything Mollie blurted out during that last time, but no one really listened to old "Molls." So it ended up as mumble jumble.

Karen often referred to her as, "Two ton Sally."

Unsure of the drug and gold flow with Jimmy and Mollie, now out of the picture, things for Karen seemed at a standstill.

She was freaking out as her husband's drug use had been eating up her profits. She only hoped that garage selling today and the following two days at the flea market would change the tide.

Quickly stepping into yesterday's clothes, Karen grabbed two packs of smokes and a Diet Coke and slipped out the back door of the single-wide trailer.

At camp, Gayle and Eden were out early with coffee and biscuits to go.

Eden was shopping for her Mother's booth as she would have little room in her return flight baggage.

At a nearby garage sale street, the two split up the street with Gayle on one side and Eden on the other.

At a more than friendly house, where an elderly couple sat in the shade, Eden picked up an antique jewelry box filled with treasures, and no sooner than had she placed a piece in her palm to examine it, it was snagged right from her hands.

From across the street, Gayle could hear her daughter's raised voice. But it wasn't a normal Eden voice, it was strong deep and commanding.

"Set it down, Bertha!"

As Gayle rushed across the street, she came face to face with her daughter and Karen fighting over the box.

While she tried to intervene, her daughter waved her on and said, "This is my fight."

The elderly woman, who was running the sale, stood up and walked over to the two women fighting about it and took the box away from Karen, and gave it back to Eden.

The woman said in Karen's direction, "I would rather donate it and sell it than to this lowlife. She's been at my sales many times. Fool me once, and you know the rest of the saying…"

Gayle and Eden smiled at one another and then gave thanks the woman for stepping in. Then the Mother and Daughter team got into their car and then busted out laughing.

"Just like old times Mum," said Eden

Gayle looked at her daughter and said, "Where are you channeling your inner roller derby queen from? Set it down, Bertha!"

The two started to laugh again until they cried. It was a day they would remember for sure.

Karen, on the other hand, got into her car pissed off. She couldn't believe that she lost out to that girl. Lighting up a cigarette, she placed it between her lips, cursing between drags, and drove out of the neighborhood.

The rest of the day didn't get much better from sale to sale.

Karen felt she was just five minutes behind all the good stuff. "Have any handbags?"

The replies were all the same, "Nope, just sold them, jewelry nope, perfume nope."

It had been a long time since she felt this desperate. So much so that she felt a good cry coming on but quickly shut that emotion off, by lighting another cigarette.

When she returned to the trailer, it wasn't because she was done, but because she couldn't afford to use any more gas finding nothing.

As she rounded the corner, the police were sitting out in front of the trailer. She would've kept driving, but they knew her car, and that would just make it look worse.

After parking her car, she got out and walked up to Bobby Burgess to see what he wanted.

Without a "Hello" or anything, Bobby said, "Karen Beckwith, you are wanted for questioning in the murders of Jimmy Smith and Mollie Highland."

He continued, "I also have a search warrant to search your trailer, as the two officers followed her inside her humble digs.

Karen dropped her cigarette on the ground and squashed it into the dirt like a bug.

Her day just got worse!

The Flea Market Tribe
Chapter Twenty One

"The Gala"

Bobby called his Mother to tell her about the arrest of
Karen.

Lee told Bobby that nothing surprised her with all of this.

She then asked him if he had had any more contact with
Eden.

Bobby said not yet, but he planned to go to the flea market
the next day.

Lee hung up the phone and conference called Jillian and
Gayle to give them the update about Karen's arrest.

She told the girls that when the police contacted Karen's
husband, he showed little interest in his wife's arrest.

Gayle, who was bubbling over with news, filled them in
about Eden's run-in with Karen.

All three women couldn't help but laugh over Eden's
spunky responses.

Gayle said she had an incoming call and that it was Bobby.
So she hit the "on" button and said, "Hello?"

Surprised, Gayle never thought she would hear Bobby
Burgess stammer like a teenage boy.

After exchanging hello's, he asked if he could speak with Eden. After their short conversation, Eden bounced into the kitchen all smiles.

"Someone's got a date," she sang out.

Sitting at his desk, Johnny B picked up the phone and called Jillian. He asked her to attend the governor's event with him.

She replied that she would attend, but she would meet him at the gala.

Smiling, Johnny thought how interesting it was that he ended up in the same small town as Jillian.

When the small-time dealer Jimmy Smith had come to Boston looking for a new source, he met up with some of Johnny's people. As Jimmy's need grew, it piqued Johnny's curiosity.

Since Johnny's father was long gone and his brother had left the business over the direction he saw the company going, all the decisions fell on Johnny's shoulders.

His brother was a bit of a pansy, or that was what Johnny thought then, to divorce himself from the dirty work of the business, yet continue to reap all the financial benefits.

It was the wrong choice in Johnny's mind, but it was over 25 years ago, and he needed to let it go.

Johnny was not even sure he would recognize his brother today if he passed him on the street.

It seemed that his brother had changed his name since he didn't want to have any connection to the family.

All Johnny knew is that he had an open pipeline to fill the town with its needs for drugs, along with the rest of the state of Maine.

Hearing the news of that broad's arrest, he now had three of his problems off the streets.

Johnny smirked but knew he had a few more loose ends to tie up before returning to Boston.

He shook his head, thinking about all the people stupid enough to get involved with drugs. Something he had never done.

Then Jillian crossed his mind again. After he ran into her at the post office, his thoughts went from happiness to seeing her again and using her as a great cover, which lent legitimacy to him. Her being a longtime resident with a great reputation and all.

Stepping out with her at this Gala would only secure his position. Yes, it was true that he likely once loved her, in his own selfish way. But he had let her move on because she was young and had her whole life in front of her. In those days he was still following his father's direction, and it was no place for a nice girl.

Jillian kicked her feet up and shaking her head at the events of the day, and thinking to herself, "Maybe I should write a book? Who is there right mind would believe this crap?"

She packed her car for the two days ahead at the flea market. She needed something to get her mind off the gala on Sunday night. Even though she was going to be very tired from the market, she still agreed to go.

"Why me?" she asked herself, with all of the available women in the area. "Why not some unsuspecting gal that had no history with Him?"

The dress that she saved in her closet for special occasions was taupe, long and very classy. Not overdone as it was the dress, she had worn to her son Peyton's wedding.

Considering she could completely chicken out and not even show up, she was not about to buy a new dress. Besides, no one was more frugal than she was.

Even though morning would be here before she knew it, she climbed into bed but couldn't help think about the chaos of the last few days.

Tossing his pencil in the air, Blaine was in a "pissy" mood. Things were falling apart with his suppliers, and his business partner was riding him about cash payments.

He wished he had never teamed up with him, but he did not have access to the kind of money he was going to need, so at the time, it seemed like the perfect marriage.

The Flea Market Tribe
Chapter Twenty Two

"Cinderella I'm Not"

Blaine was pretty sure a big change was coming.

Knowing that the narcotics trade wouldn't miss a beat in
town, his major concern was the stolen jewelry. With all
the heat on regarding the murders in town, if his "trading"
dried up, it would clearly affect his own financial health.

He wanted to make sure he was getting his fair share, so
before losing out anywhere, he was going to scrub some
profits off the top of the refinery funds.

Anxious and concerned, he was not sure when the crap was
going to hit the fan, but it was coming, and he felt it was
going to take him out like a freight train.

Suddenly his office door burst open and his partner walked
in.

"WTF Blaine!!!, word has it that one of your acquaintances
from the flea market along with two other people in town
have been murdered horrifically!"

Frank continued spouting off at Blaine. "Why are you even
going there? We don't need it. We don't need that kind of
public relations nightmare!"

It looked like steam was actually permeating from his head.
Walking back out the way he came in; he slammed the door
as he left the room.

Blaine was confounded. He might need to visit his fixer.

Jillian was preparing for the evening ahead. She went for an updo on her hair with a single vintage hair clip.

Borrowing from Gayle, she slipped over her shoulders a fabulous English woven wrap that graced her middle-aged body like a princess. The drop Lucite and crystal earrings dangled stylishly from each ear.

She was nervous about going and tried to talk herself out of it several times. She called her husband who was in Athens and told him, and although he was less than pleased, he said to her, "Be careful, but have fun and a good time, then let me know how it went."

She drove to the estate and felt that tingling tummy like a schoolgirl.

As she stepped out of her car, the door was held open by the attendant, who she thanked.

Jillian then turned in the direction of the entrance, and she felt a sharp pain as she rolled her ankle in the two-inch heels.

She wanted to cry. It wasn't the first time. Still, she felt like an idiot. Who did she think she was, "Cinderella?"

She thought she could try to walk it off but decided to sit down for a minute or two.

Someone must have seen it and alerted Johnny, who was soon by her side.

"How can I help?" he asked.

He looked at her now in bare feet, high heels in hand.

He said, "I can carry you if you'd like?"

She replied, "No, Johnny, this girl is heading home."

As she fought off all his offers to drive her home, she told him it was her left foot and that she would be fine.

As she drove home, she scolded herself for even attending. Even though her husband gave his blessing, he was still concerned, and now Jillian was sure that Nicholas would chuckle at her clumsiness but be grateful that she wasn't more injured.

As she pulled up to her camp, she was glad that her truck was packed up for the flea market.

She should likely take the next day off, she told herself. But she was too stubborn, so she wrapped her ankle, after soaking it for a half hour.

This injury was not her first rodeo, so to speak. So she hung up her dress, and while making her lunch for the next day, she reexamined her simple life that she had carved out for herself.

Putting together a salad with the greens from her garden, she remembered her husband sharing the experiences to Monte Carlo. He was spending time with his artistic partner, best friend, and brother by choice and his lovely wife. They would go to the market and only buy what was in season. The descriptions and the photographs made me want to emulate the same thing here — the simplicity of life.

Not long after his last visit, his best friend who had been suffering health wise ended his physical walk on earth. But he was still everywhere, in the music and novels he wrote and played, and his love that everyone still felt.

My husband had taken it very hard. Art was the person he spoke with every day and bounced ideas off. Both guys would talk about history, and when Nickolas started telling me about his findings or some other historic or travel thing, I would often say to him, "I was making up my shopping list in my head, Darling. What did you say?"

Nickolas would just laugh, and that was that.

Jillian tried to be her husband's sounding board, but she could never fill the void. So he ramped up the frequency of his trips, and she understood. Time was slipping away, and she knew with every step he now took, he was carrying Art on a new adventure, to places his wheelchair couldn't.

The Flea Market Tribe
Chapter Twenty Two

"Karen's Days were Numbered"

With Karen in custody, and her husband hiding out, the cops had their hands full.

She was crying foul, that she was innocent and her husband was her alibi, but the police placed her in the local lockup among women.

Karen knew that she led a dirty and tricky past.

Both she and her husband had shorted many on the drug deals, mainly because her husband was now hooked on most of what they traded.

Being incarcerated was not something new to Karen. She had a rap sheet dating back to her fourteen birthday.

Though she had been more cautious lately as she had so much more to lose, it was still more than what she had bargained for.

The first night in she got in a fight and ended with a black eye and a big fat lip. The inmate was someone Karen knew when she was working the corner for quick fixes.

The first thing the green haired woman said to Karen was, "I can't believe someone would pay to get with that! I guess the fetish community? The Craigslist killer saw your ad and ran away Karen? Your own husband wants no part of that stank! That's why he switched teams, Karen?"

Before she could process all of her words, the large woman was on her like chipped beef on toast.

The two feisty females fight was quickly broken up by a couple of female guards but not before Karen was the one bleeding.

Karen prayed that her man would come forward, but she had a very uneasy feeling and wanted to get released as fast as possible.

She couldn't sleep; she was too afraid that she would be stuck in there for something she didn't do.

The morning arrived, and she had not even closed her eyes. It was a no smoking jail, and she felt she was going to lose her shit. Everything and everybody was pissing her off.

When they got called for chow, the breakfast looked disgusting and smelled like the inside of the shared toilet in the cell.

Karen couldn't stomach it and just drank coffee.

Her state provided attorney informed Karen that the police were coming to interview her.

"More like interrogate," she thought.

The attorney then told her, "Unless they have additional evidence against you, Karen, they will let you go. The charges for the small amount of drug paraphernalia found was minor and the jewelry they found, they were running through their system to ensure it was not stolen. So don't worry!"

But Karen was. As the day dragged on, Karen had received only one visitor, her husband's guy pal Freddy.

He said to her, "Your husband only wants to know if you sold him out, and was there any money hidden anywhere."

Karen sat with her mouth wide open, nicotine-stained teeth not believing what he just asked her and then collapsed on the table after suffering a massive widow maker.

Freddy started screaming for help as she slumped forward.

It was over as quickly as it started. Some would later say Karen got what she deserved, however as much as she was disliked, no one deserved to die that way.

The Flea Market Tribe
Chapter Twenty Three

"Fast Fashion Frock"

Jillian shook her head as she walked around the garage sale area of the flea market. Each booth had piles of clothing.

The decluttering trends are good and healthy, but the "fast fashion garments," which are lower quality items, are worn an average of only seven times before donating, or worse being thrown away.

Society and its extremely disposable fashions are the trends today. Want to improve your carbon, water, and waste footprint? If you're going to purchase something, make sure it is better quality, or purchase quality items second hand.

Jillian was walking slowly due to the bandaged ankle.

Finding the fruit booths, she picked up bananas and a few other items she didn't grow in her garden. She always traveled with her cooler, not only for her lunch but also to add fresh items from the produce stands.

One area that she never missed was to shop the booths of the "Extreme Couponers." (slang word).

She could always find some nice deals, and even better ones if they have an overage or "Best Buy" date that was nearing. Those dates meant nothing to Jillian. Frugality, at its best, was her motto.

She finally made her way back to her booth just as the news of Karen's death was hitting the flea market.

She didn't know why she was so shocked. She seemed invincible. In her mind, Karen was the wicked witch from the Wizard of Oz, as the scene "I'm melting" kept replaying in her mind.

Karen had tormented Jillian and every other person she came in contact with. Now it was the end of an era. Her reign was over.

Thomas appeared in shock, sitting in his foldable chair.

I knew he was likely in the early stages of dementia or something similar, but this was different, he was clearly stunned.

Slouched in the metal chair, with his hands holding up his head, Thomas couldn't speak. He wasn't sad; she was a horrible person. Yet he was terrified.

He was afraid for himself. It meant that all of the plates he had spinning in the air were about to come crashing down on his head and his life, but more importantly... his wife.

"Everything was going fine before he got involved with Karen and her group," he cursed silently.

He had become so used to all the money, that once it started only to trickle in, he was into deep, purchasing a new pool, the outdoor grilling kitchen, and upgrading his cars. It was a way to bury the extra cash.

He had gotten to the point where he had taken a few short term loans out with Blaine. Loans that he feared he may now default on.

As the top cop of the town continued his morning rounds, Bobby Burgess jumped out of his police-issued truck and kicked the dirt off his boots and entered the gravel-lined flea market walkways.

He was greeted by vendors, flea market staff, and shoppers.

He headed towards the booths of his Mom and the Flea Market Tribe, but most importantly, to meet Eden.

Entering the covered area, he immediately saw her.

She was dressed in denim Capri high waisted trousers and a sleeveless white linen shirt that tied just above her flat stomach.

The red nautical hoop earrings that her Mum had given her were vintage Kenneth Jay Lane and twinkled in the sunlight.

Helping the three women, Eden was now in Jillian's booth as she rested her foot.

Eden was finishing up with a customer when Bobby walked in. He hugged all the ladies and headed towards Eden. They were going out that night, and it almost seemed they had known each other for years rather than days.

Smiling like children at each other and unsure what to do next, Eden walked up to Bobby then wrapped her arms around him tightly, almost hugging the air out of his lungs.

Us three Moms, stood there with jaws dropped. You would have thought that these two lovebirds were long lost, friends.

Then she said, "And hello to you!"

Bobby was melting inside and sweating outside.

When they parted their embrace, it was like "fairy dust" was illuminating from their bodies.

The Moms just stood there, stunned till Dean, the record guy said, "Really, could you please get them a room or something!"

His comment broke us all up as we then gathered around and chatted like geese on a farm.

In the parking lot to the south entrance, Johnny B parked his BMW in a spot for handicap parking, then placed his Massachusetts issued placard in the window.

Johnny didn't normally walk through flea markets much less dirt. He stopped one of the associates to find out where Jilly's booth was.

He had driven by Jillian's house when he got into town and saw that her truck was gone and no one was home.

He couldn't believe she'd gone to the market. "God," he thought. "If she needed money, he would have given it to her!"

Knowing she would never accept it, he just thought that to be nice.

Walking down the aisle where her booth was located, he noticed that it was full. Jillian, her two friends, a young woman and a tall man in a windbreaker, was standing there in a huddle it seemed.

"Hello!!! Are we having fun yet?" Johnny said with all the Johnny B bravado he could muster.

He exchanged greetings with the group and was introduced to Eden, Gayle's daughter, and Bobby, Lee's son.

Jillian was embarrassed that Johnny had shown up there and even more so as he began to recount how the injury occurred.

As Bobby stood there listening, he couldn't help wondering what this guy's angle was, and who he was. Bobby had encountered him in town and thought he was a tourist.

Jillian blurted out as Johnny went on, "But I'm going to acupuncture tomorrow!"

Everyone turned and looked at her.

"Hey, it works!" Jillian stated.

Johnny B took Jillian's arm and motioned to walk outside the booth to where the cars were parked behind the stalls.

He then asked her if he could call her later.

Jillian said yes, but only because she was going to pull the plug on their friendship as it was just feeling very wrong.

When Johnny left, Bobby asked Jillian, "What in the world are you doing with that clown? Who is he? It is so unlike you, Jillian."

Jillian brushed Bobby off and told him he was only an old family friend, and there was nothing more to it.

Bobby wasn't so sure. Before he left, he told Eden that he looked forward to seeing her later that afternoon.

As Bobby drove through the parking area, he saw Johnny walking to a black sedan parked in the handicapped spot. He pulled his truck over and asked him what exactly his disability was?

Johnny looked surprised but answered sarcastically and said, "What exactly makes it your business?"

Bobby immediately pulled out his badge.

He replied, "Everything that goes on in this town is my business, including the woman you are showing interest in. My aunt has been married for a long time, and although her husband is traveling, he's very much in the picture.

Johnny smoothly backed down from his tone and said, "You've got it all wrong man."

Bobby said, "Ok," as he noted Johnny's plate number.

"I'll be looking into that, Johnny."

The Flea Market Tribe
Chapter Twenty Four

"Bobby and Johnny"

Johnny headed into town. He was meeting a real estate
appraiser. He was interested in some property and was
hopeful that he would see more of Jillian.

Not looking for anything serious but Johnny always
thought that Jillian was a looker.

He wasn't too worried about her husband, and he obviously
wasn't too worried about his wife, since he was constantly
traveling.

After paying for his lunch, he used the restroom then
walked around the corner to his car. There in front of his
eyes, his car was now in an angled position dangling from
the tow truck.

He couldn't believe it and ran up to the truck window and
started beating on it.

"What, what, what's your problem?" the tow driver
stuttered and screamed.

"Your towing my car...man!"

Johnny saw that the towing bar was dragging the back end
of his car and scrapping the bumper.

"Well," said the driver, "You're parked in a handicapped
spot."

"I have tags for that," said Johnny.

Walking up behind Johnny, Bobby Burgess halfway smiled and said, "Well not a legal tag! Yours was a tag that you were gifted through political favor. I'm sure if you are truly disabled, you can bring your medical records in front of our local judge. But for the time being, your car is being towed to the impound lot. You can pick it up there and pay the fine, and be sure to bring cash now since we don't accept checks."

The tow truck finally got the car in the correct position and drove off, with Bobby following him to the impound lot.

Johnny was beyond pissed.

"This guy was messing with me," Johnny thought to himself. "He is most certainly unaware of who I am!"

Standing there on the sidewalk, trying to decide what to do, Johnny thought more about the situation. "It's not like he was going to have this cop discretely removed. But it did make his presence in town a little more awkward, being on the watchlist, by this Disneyland patrolman. He might need to re-think the whole small town idea."

At Gayle's camp, Eden got dressed for her date with Bobby. She was very excited. When it normally took her 25 minutes to get ready, today it took her an hour and a half.

She enjoyed the long bubble bath, adding the light makeup and springy curls that when she pulled her fingers through them, it left a sensual looking wave.

Her dress was soft lilac in color, and she wore strappy sandals.

Arriving at the prescribed time, Bobby picked her up, and they were off.

First, he took her to every special place in town, every spot that he had his "first" times. This included the first time he rode his bike somewhere alone. The first movie he ever went to, and then a picnic overlooking the lake.

At dusk, they used flashlights. They drank sparkling wine out of paper cups and laughed.

When Bobby drove Eden home, he ran around the side of the car and opened her door. He then held her hand as he walked her up to the screened enclosure.

He kissed her lightly and said, "I hope to see you tomorrow."

Eden smiled and said, "Yes, me too." Then she floated into the house, meanwhile telling the little girl inside her, "Don't get too ahead of yourself here!"

Making his way back to his truck, Bobby sat there for a moment, before starting the engine and flipping on the country music station.

As he pulled onto the main road away from the camp, he smiled, turned the music up and started singing cheesy country songs all the way home.

The next few days went by fast for everyone involved.

Between showing Eden around, Gayle was competing with Bobby for her daughter's time.

Gayle knew how happy her daughter was but was worried about how it was going to affect her when it was time to leave.

Eden sat with Gayle, and they discussed the status of the Tea Room, along with some possible new products that Gayle was suggesting to Eden. Then Gayle asked her daughter, "Have you considered selling it and moving here? I would love to have you living here with me. Besides, you and Bobby have such a lovely thing going; don't you want to see where it goes?"

"Mum," Eden said, "He is a terrific man, and I am having the time of my life getting to know him. Do I think I could fall in love with him? Certainly."

"But" she started to say when Gayle gave her the motherly look

"Oh, that dreaded But word?" Gayle asked.

Eden shushed her Mother.

"Mum, I'm not about to sell the Tea Room that I have spent nearly every day of my life, for a man...Any man."

Gayle then responded, "My dear daughter, I know you are afraid to put yourself out there like that. However, you should at least think about it, please?"

Eden agreed, but she knew that she couldn't sell or leave her life and the Tea Room.

Her mind drifted to the step stool that was in the Tea Room kitchen, where she had stood like a little wavy haired girl with light blue cat eye shaped glasses.

She thought about standing on the step stool wearing burnt orange vintage "whomper stomper" boots she had begged her Mother for, saying she would wear them to school every day and forgetting that more than half of her wardrobe included dresses.

So there she would stand on the step stool, wearing a dress, knee-high white socks, and those whomper stompers.

It's not that kids don't get picked on enough in school, but Eden held her head up high and told herself she was a trendsetter and future style icon.

Living together in that small town, Eden loved her Mother very much and hoped one day she would meet someone so that she wouldn't be alone.

Now her Mum lives in the United States and is still single after all these years, but does date from time to time, so just maybe one day she will meet someone nice to marry again.

Gayle's longtime pen pal and best friend Lee was over the moon. Her son had finally made a connection with someone. It helped that it was her best friend's daughter.

The two old hens were already planning their wedding. They were even caught a few times, sending each other text messages while everyone was in the car.

"Mothers that want grandchildren are a fierce bunch!" I would tell Gayle and Lee.

When the Palm Beach County Coroners office called early that morning, Lee answered the phone.

The woman on the other end of the line said that she was searching for information on the next of kin for Roger Burgess.

Lee sat down.

"He was dead?"

The man at the helm of everything bad that ever happened to her was dead.

She began to cry. Not tears of sadness but relief and sheer happiness, to finally be free.

She asked why they were not in touch with his current wife June.

The corners assistance, Elaine said, "She would have the local police involved contact her."

Lee asked if it was natural and was told the autopsy was inconclusive.

An hour later the Palm Beach Sheriff's Department called, and Lee spoke with Deputy Beaupre.

He told her that even though the coroner deemed it inconclusive, it looked natural. He was found slumped over a glass of scotch.

His wife June was not there. It appeared she had moved out, but they were unaware of the timeline.

They wanted to contact Bobby, but Lee asked if she could tell him herself?

The Sheriff asked Lee, "Sure, can you please have Bobby contact me, Deputy Beaupre, as a professional courtesy?"

He then said, "Thank you, ma'am, I will be waiting for his call."

Sitting on her couch, Lee reminisced. She found living alone to be a punishment since early on; she had lived the life of a princess, that ended with her marriage.

A small curl of a smile crossed her lips; she was free forever.

Bobby was busy at the station. With Karen dead, the two murder cases were still open as she had never actually been charged with either of them.

The police needed to find her husband and interrogate him. Hopefully, he could help put some of the pieces together.

Just because Bobby was balls to the walls busy, didn't mean that Eden wasn't on his mind because she was.

He was head over heels, and his thoughts were many including, "Now that he found her, how was he going to let her get on an airplane in five short days and fly away from him?"

Just then, Bobby's private cell phone rang. It was his Mother.

"Yes, Mom?" he answered.

Lee asked if he could stop by on her way home.

He asked if it could wait till tomorrow?

She said, "No."

Cruising through the wooded area of town, Blaine figured he needed to make contact with the stranger that showed up at the flea market.

He dropped off a card at the motel with Hannah, who was the front desk clerk. He wanted to know who the shiny black BMW belonged to that was parked in front. He had seen this car before and wanted to meet the gentleman that owned it.

Blaine had a suspicion who the man was, J. Burton, as he smooth talked Hannah into giving Blaine his name.

Now, he needed to see if Mr. Burton would show up at Delmonico's and drove there the long way to wait.

An hour later, Blaine ordered a Manhattan, sitting at the bar.

When Johnny left the motel gym, he walked across the lobby. He had a lot of bad jujus to burn off. He had spent an extra hour and a half at the impound lot retrieving his car, which really made him angry.

As he was about to step onto the elevator, Hannah called out his name, "Mr. Burton!"

Hannah ran around the counter and gave Johnny a card and told him that it was delivered for him just a short while ago.

Johnny taking the card, thanked Hannah, and headed up to his room.

After reading the card a couple of times, he thought, "Really interesting turn of events" and headed into the shower.

An hour later, Johnny walked into Delmonico's, where the restaurant and bar were full of well-dressed people enjoying themselves.

Johnny thought to himself, "See these people know how to have fun."

He saw a man waving at him in a corner.

Walking to the table, Johnny was greeted with "Mr. Burton," Blaine said. "I can't tell you how good it is to connect."

Johnny said, "Thank you, I have recently found out that we have a few people in common."

Just then, the bartender approached, and Johnny ordered a Cabernet, as he sat down.

The two men then began with some small talk that led to where they had lived, what kind of work they did, etc.

Both men were rather chatty.

Blaine told Johnny without revealing details that he had some special work that needed to be done. Plus Blaine needed this person to be discreet.

Johnny said he might find someone that he could contact and would let Blaine know in a few days.

Then they went right back to discussing Boston, The Red Sox, and women.

The restaurant was hopping, and a small jazz duo played in the corner.

When they went their separate ways that night, Blaine told himself that the meeting was a success. He felt he'd known Johnny for years, while still respectfully noting to himself that Johnny Burton was a very dangerous man.

Blaine still had Thomas to deal with, especially his outstanding loans. He could definitely use the influx of cash right now and wondered if Thomas could ante up any of the money now.

Heading home, Blaine was hopeful that the meeting with Johnny would sort out his professional as well as financial issues. It's not that he wanted to have his partner Frank killed, but options were running slim to none.

Blaine hoped that J. Burton could pull a rabbit out of his hat on his situation.

Across town, Bobby was pulling into the drive to his Mother's camp. The light was on the front porch.

He could clearly see the outline of her Mother sitting on the antique white rocker.

He walked up and sat in the matching chair. Lee offered him a glass of wine.

As she sipped her ice-cold Kendall Jackson Chardonnay, she hoped this wouldn't be a difficult conversation.

As she began to speak the words just tumbled out.

When she was done, Bobby poured them each another glass. Then Bobby raised his and said, "To surviving Roger Burgess."

As they clinked their glasses and smiled at one another, Bobby thought he heard the crystal clink echo all the way down the street.

The Flea Market Tribe
Chapter Twenty Five

"Gino"

Johnny put a call into Gino and asked him to come and visit
him in the small town that he saw as a possible place for
good business.

Gino had been with Johnny B since they spent their
summers on the Falmouth Heights beaches.

The three were friends and roommates, the Brothers Burton
and Gino.

They worked hard but played even harder. They were
definitely "man whores" tapping most of the tourist girls
and several locals. However, they tried to steer clear of the
Cape Cod girls as they were too close for comfort.

Gino packed his blue Corvette and was pretty jazzed about
getting out of Boston for a few days and away from his
wife, Anna. She had been all up in his business since
retiring from the school system.

Gino chuckled out loud, driving across the Bunker Hill
Memorial Bridge. "Yep," he thought, "Gino, the fixer and
the old schoolmarm."

The drive was nice, and the sound system in the "Vette"
was primo.

It was a five-hour cruise, with good tunes blasting, and the
perfect joint to smoke, as he made his way to see his old
friend. By the time he arrived, Gino was feeling pretty
chill and ready to help Johnny in any way he could.

He had booked a room at the motel across from Johnny. Better not to be connected just in case.

Gino grabbed a meal and hit the hay early since he assumed tomorrow would be a busy one.

It was nearly 8 PM as Blaine had set up a meeting with Thomas. He needed to straighten out the financial issues between the two. They had enjoyed a good run, but now Thomas was just becoming a liability.

Meanwhile, Thomas was fearful about getting together with Blaine. He knew from past experiences that Blaine's temper was not only bad but almost evil. He wasn't sure what he could say or do for Blaine to satisfy the loan.

Thomas kept thinking, "Was there a temporary fix, or even more time to repay the money?"

The two met at the diner in town and sat at the counter.

Blaine said, "Thomas, naturally, you are aware that we have some problems. Not only has our status changed in the way we did business together, but you also have a financial situation to figure out."

Thomas looked at Blaine straight in the eye and said, "I am an old man. I am likely going to lose my home, and when that happens likely my wife of 40 years. When she finds out what a mess I have made, no woman, even one as loyal as she, is going to get past all the lies and all the thievery. I don't know what else to do."

Blaine looked at the older man. Just a shadow of what he once was. Then he told him, "Remove the two gold rings, the neck chain, the link bracelet and watch."

Thomas started to remove his wedding ring, and Blaine stopped him and said, "I'm not that callous of a man."

Blaine then instructed Thomas to stay away from the flea market, "Call it health-related retirement."

Thomas asked, "Are we even now and done?"

Blaine smiled and said, "Yes, as long as you remain silent and out of sight."

Then Blaine walked out of the diner, feeling confident that that issue was solved.

Blaine convinced himself that even though he took a financial hit since the jewelry was simply pennies on the dollar, it was worth its weight in gold to tie up loose ends and move in the direction of the real problem.

At the edge of town, Johnny and Gino met at the motel gym. They appeared to be just two guys working out and sharing a conversation.

Johnny gave the details to Gino.

During the rest of the workout, the two guys commiserated about their youth, the trouble that the three of them would get into and getting caught up with their lives.

Gino asked if there had been any word about his brother?

Johnny told him, "I really don't want to talk about it. He had made his choice and left Johnny to deal with their Father and the business. So we went our separate ways, and that was that!"

Gino asked Johnny for the name of the intended mark.

Johnny told him that he never even asked. He didn't want to know. He was Blaine's business partner and spent most of his life behind his desk, or that's what was said.

Over the next few days, Gino went on recon and setting up a plan to present to Blaine.

Jillian, on the other hand, was extremely busy with the flea market and her girls.

Jillian's garden was overproducing, so the girls got together with Mason jars and did some canning. It felt so natural to be with her tribe.

She couldn't help love the fact that they were using canning jars that were lovingly discarded by someone who no longer felt their worth.

Eden was out with Bobby, and the women enjoyed discussing the lovebirds.

Lee and Gayle were talking hopeful future weddings and grandchildren. Both were also very worried if Eden returned home without giving their relationship a proper chance.

Gayle shared the conversation she and Eden had regarding the Tea Room. All three ladies were trying to stay hopeful.

Jillian told the group that she was happy that all was quiet and she had not heard from Johnny B.

Unfortunately, Lee filled her in about the run in between Bobby and Johnny.

Gayle said, "Johnny B will never change. He had just been schmoozing her with his "I'm just a good guy, bologna," she thought. "Once a jerk, always a jerk," as she finished her comment.

For Eden and Bobby, it was closing in on "D" day, as they tried to come up with a reasonable solution.

Bobby told Eden, "I'm sorry baby, there is nothing reasonable when love is involved."

They had to laugh when simultaneously they both commented that that's the exact reason they had run in the other direction when it came to love.

Eden needed to get back to her Mother's as they had an early morning flea market, which would be her last before returning to her home in England and the life that she had put on hold.

Bobby drove her home and walked her to her door.

He kissed the lips of the girl he was falling in love with and left. He thought he knew what was to become of them.

Pulling away from the curb, Bobby got a call from the police, two towns over.

They had arrested Karen's husband and his partner during a drug sting. They were holding them for Bobby.

Being late and the arresting officers just ending their shifts, they made plans to collect the suspects the next morning. Bobby felt like he had not slept in days and was only too willing to go home and crash out for the night.

Outside the motel, Gino had packed his suitcase and placed it behind his seat in the small area, that was only large enough for a dog or child. His trunk was used only for necessities.

Then he drove to the office building that Blaine occupied with his business partner.

As he parked out front, he saw a tall stranger walking out of the building. He followed him and watched him walk into the post office to retrieve mail from his post office box.

As Gino watched him through the military binocular's, the man turned, and the light hit his face just right. It was Frank. Frank Burton. His childhood friend, Johnny's brother.

Closing his eyes, he knew he had a job to do, and as he lifted his cell phone to call Johnny, he pushed it to end the call.

If Frank spent his whole life running, how could Gino possibly tell Johnny that Frank was the target?

Gino drove the car out of the lot.

He called Blaine and asked if they could meet up.

Gino told him to meet him out in front of Delmonaco's, and he'd pick him up there.

Once Blaine received a call, he was certain that Gino wanted to give him the final details and to give Gino the envelope of cash.

When Gino drove around the corner in the shiny midnight blue Corvette, he saw the man that Johnny had described and stopped. Even before Gino met Blaine, he knew it was him.

Blaine was impressed with the car.

Smiling, Blaine stuck his head into the open window, and Gino said, "Jump in, let's go for a ride."

Blaine followed his new friend's direction, and after closing the door, Gino hit the gas pedal, and they were off.

When Blaine ask Gino where they were going, Gino replied, "Hope you don't mind that we need to drive a while, but I've got an errand to do. We're going to celebrate, of course, since everything is already done!"

Blaine was stunned, then nervous, but happy that his situation was already better. So he handed Gino the envelope of cash and said, "Thank You!"

Gino replied with a smile and placed the money in the glove box.

Knowing that it would take another five hours to drive back, Gino strung Blaine along with small talk and listening to the great sound system playing "The Eagles."

In Gino's mind, the music was creating the soundtrack for what was to happen.

Stopping halfway for a couple of shots at one of Gino's "easy going biker bar," Blaine was becoming boisterous and grinning like a schoolgirl. He was throwing money around like he had a never-ending supply.

As they jumped back in the "Vette," Gino lit up a joint and continued the drive. At some point, Blaine fell asleep, and Gino continued his ride to the Cape.

They arrived at about 3:30 AM in Falmouth at a yard where he flashed his high beams to open the gate.

Gino pulled the car into the heavy equipment garage, which belonged to the local trash compactor company. As he stepped out of his pride possession, there stood his hefty "Portuguese" friend with his signature black and grey beard.

As the two men walked together towards the "Vette," Gino could see that Blaine was now standing beside the car, shaking off his nap.

"Why are we here, Gino?" Blaine asked.

Gino replied that his friend needed some help with some equipment, and since he knew how to work it from his younger days, he was always happy to help.

The three men then walked in the direction of a very large piece of equipment.

As they stood alongside it, Gino, who was almost as large as his friend said, "Dude, I'll never fit, I've gotten too fat in my old age."

His friend laughed and said, "That's my problem too."

Gino then looked at Blaine and asked him if he thought he could reach in and flip the switch.

Blaine initially complained, "Hey, I'm not here to work. I'm here to celebrate, remember?"

Gino quickly said, "No problem. We will. I just need you to help me out here, OK. Just reach in and pull the switch?"

"OK," replied Blaine, "All right, I will."

Blaine shrugged his shoulders and wondered why he ended up being the "helpful hardware guy"? However, he agreed to do it so that he could get away from what was reeking around this giant piece of metal.

As he climbed up into the machine, the smell started to gag him, and as he reached for the switch, Gino pushed him in.

The Portuguese immediately tapped the outside switch, and the compactor began to demolish its contents.

Gino halfway smiled and said, "He'll never be found!"

"Nope," the man replied. "Our motto should be, sometimes the trash takes itself out."

Knowing that his job was done, Gino stepped back into his car and headed for Boston.

Keeping friends as friends, Gino decided as he was driving back home that he would never tell Johnny about his brother. He would only tell Johnny that the job was complete. Gino owed it to Frank, to keep him secluded.

The next morning Johnny woke to Gino's cryptic but directly to the point message and decided to head back to Boston for a few days himself.

Rather than stir up anything else in the town, he wouldn't say goodbye to Jillian as he would probably be back before she knew he was gone anyway.

Johnny packed up his bags, showered, then dressed and made his way out of town before most people had woken up. It was going to be a great day.

An early call to Bobby from the police holding the two clowns, one being Karen's husband came as a surprise.

It appeared that while eating breakfast in the general population chow hall, both men were shanked in what they called a one-sided fight. In other words, they were taken out.

Since it was in their jurisdiction, they had the indubitable job to process all the paperwork.

Bobby felt like his day was going to get worse from here on out.

He was going to pick up Eden and take her to breakfast, then pick up the rest of the ladies to escort Eden to the airport. It was going to be a nightmare he felt.

As they sat holding hands in the diner that he had likely eaten a thousand meals in his lifetime and the place where he had many of his firsts, Eden and he made a plan.

When they left the diner, they went to see the "Three Hens" impatiently waiting for them.

As Bobby announced that Eden would not be leaving today, tears and cheers came from the three women.

But then he told them that Eden's flight had been delayed a week and they all gave him the sad face.

Then he said, "Listen, I've decided to arrange a leave of absence and go with Eden and see if we might establish our life together there."

As happy as Lee was for her son, she sobbed. Only she didn't tell him it was because she would be lonely.

However, he deserved to go and live his own life.

When Jillian asked him, "How can you leave with all the open-ended questions with what it happened in town?"

"Aunt Jillian," Bobby said, "Amazingly enough, they have resolved themselves for now."

Then everyone hugged and embraced.

While the three older women promised to visit Eden and Bobby in the Tea room, the morning Maine sunlight was shining brighter than it had ever done before.

The Flea Market Tribe
Chapter Twenty-Six

"Conclusion"

Thinking to herself, Jillian sat in her bathrobe, drinking her tea. She promised herself that she would have no more to do with Johnny. That was a lifetime ago and no need to re-energize something that would go nowhere.

With the last several months filled with chaos from crime, drugs, murder and the real emotional love between Eden and Bobby, it was time to get back to what she knew best, The Flea Market!

Just as she turned the page on the latest "Country Living," Jillian was startled with the loud thud that occurred on the front door.

As the doorknob turned clockwise, Jillian moved quietly and in the direction of her firearm. There in the doorway stood a man who was removing his hat.

Looking at the shadow, she didn't know who could have come in so easily, then a light was switched on, and she heard a voice, "Did I miss anything?" her husband asked.